Love Lucy

By

L.E. Saunders

MAPLE
PUBLISHERS

Love Lucy ♡

Author: L.E. Saunders

Copyright © L.E. Saunders 2025

The right of L.E. Saunders to be identified as author of this work has been asserted by the author in accordance with section 77 and 78 of the Copyright, Designs and Patents Act 1988.

First Published in 2025

ISBN 978-1-83538-641-5 (Paperback)
      978-1-83538-642-2 (E-Book)

Book Cover Design and Book Layout by:
      White Magic Studios
      www.whitemagicstudios.co.uk

Published by:
      Maple Publishers
      Fairbourne Drive, Atterbury,
      Milton Keynes,
      MK10 9RG, UK
      www.maplepublishers.com

A CIP catalogue record for this title is available from the British Library.

DEDICATION

I would like to dedicate this book to my wonderful children, Daniel, James, and Winter. To my cherished grandchildren, Lacey-Mai, Faye, and River, and to the love of my life, Lloyd.

ACKNOWLEDGEMENT

A heartfelt thank you to Laura Lucas for the beautiful book image and to Bethany Saunders for her unwavering support.

Chapter One

Lucy DeMarco was raised in an average suburban family, where the warmth of family dinners and lively discussions filled their home. Her parents balanced their professional lives with the demands of raising two children. David, her father, worked as a high school teacher, while her mother, Karen, juggled multiple roles as a part-time nurse and an active volunteer in the community. Their steady presence created a foundation of security and love.

Lucy's relationship with her older brother, Dale, was both a source of comfort and constant challenge for her. Their close bond manifested in shared laughter and memories, but there were often spirited debates that could escalate into full-fledged sibling rivalries. These arguments, driven by their distinct personalities, often revolved around topics like relationships, career aspirations, and even trivial matters like music preferences. Despite these occasional conflicts, Lucy valued Dale's perspective, especially given his experiences with women that left him wary and reluctant to pursue lasting relationships. After a couple of painful breakups, Dale embraced the single life, opting for a carefree lifestyle filled with adventurous outings and spontaneous decisions.

Their parents, while not excessively involved in their children's personal choices, always stayed tuned in to the day-to-day happenings in their lives. They would engage in friendly conversations, sharing wisdom and anecdotes from their own youthful indiscretions, though they often emphasised that Lucy and Dale were now adults capable of making their own decisions—even if those decisions sometimes led to learning hard life lessons.

While Lucy loved the idea of forging her own identity, she also enjoyed the occasional light-hearted discussions with her parents, seeing it as an avenue to share her own thoughts and experiences. Their insights, though sometimes perceived as meddling, provided her with food for thought without ever compromising her autonomy. She considered herself a free spirit, someone who thrived on creativity and self-expression, often making bold choices that matched her adventurous personality. Having navigated a labyrinth of missteps before reaching her thirties, Lucy had become resolute in her convictions. The scars of her past—each mistake a chapter in her personal history—had taught her the invaluable art of self-reliance. She now carried herself with a quiet confidence, passionately believing that her journey was uniquely hers and that taking advice from others would be a betrayal of her hard-earned wisdom.

For Lucy, the thrill of making her own choices, whether right or wrong, was essential to her growth. She felt that by allowing others to dictate her path, she would risk stunting her ability to hone her decision-making skills, which she regarded as vital tools for her future.

Lucy was undoubtedly an uncommon decision-maker, especially when it came to the intricacies of her life choices. She had been entrenched in a relationship for the past twelve years—one that, while rooted in friendship, had devolved into a routine devoid of romantic affection. They shared laughter, inside jokes, and cherished memories, but beneath the surface lay a stark absence of love that lingered like an uninvited guest. It was a companionship that offered warmth and familiarity, yet it fell short of the passionate connection she once dreamed of.

Years earlier, after enduring a series of tumultuous experiences and heartbreaks that left her feeling vulnerable, Lucy had made a conscious choice to pursue a life of tranquillity. The tumult of seeking romance had worn her down, and she found herself disenchanted with the fairytale concept of "prince charming." After countless encounters that fizzled before they could blossom, she reached a sombre realisation: perhaps such a figure was nothing more than a figment of her imagination, and if he did exist, she had neither the patience nor the energy to seek him out.

Throughout the years, Lucy had turned down a string of marriage proposals, each one presented with hopeful eyes by suitors she simply did not love. She believed that genuine love was a necessity for such a binding commitment; anything less felt like a betrayal to herself. The notion of comfort took precedence in her mind—she reasoned that as long as she felt secure and at ease in her daily life, which was more than sufficient. The allure of romance paled in comparison to the stability she had cultivated, and in her heart, she accepted her unconventional path, finding solace in the knowledge that true love, while a lovely notion, wasn't the only route to a fulfilling life.

Lucy's career decisions were a stark contrast to her relationship status; they were marked by a spontaneity that often took her by surprise. With an insatiable drive, she would pinpoint a career path—sometimes a fledgling idea bursting with potential—and throw herself into it with relentless determination. She would climb the ladder, often reaching impressive heights, only to abruptly pivot and embark on a completely new adventure in an entirely different field. This whirlwind of career transitions painted a vivid picture of her professional life, yet beneath it all lay a singular dream that persisted through her chaotic journey: to own her own business.

Living a contemporary lifestyle, Lucy envisioned a life that mirrored the societal milestones many around her seemed to achieve effortlessly—a devoted partner to share her adventures with, a cosy home filled with warmth and laughter, a sleek car that expressed her individuality, and the financial security to enjoy life without the weight of worry. In the back of her mind lingered the idea of children, dreams of nurturing a little family one day, but even more profound was her longing to travel.

The world was a vast canvas, vibrant and teeming with cultures she yearned to witness firsthand. Yet, amidst her countless career changes, Lucy had neglected to carve out the time to truly explore it. Each decision felt like a stepping stone, but instead of leading her directly to her aspirations, they often diverted her path. As a result, she found herself grappling with a collection of unfulfilled dreams and the haunting feeling that she had settled for second best.

Lucy had traversed a myriad of professional landscapes over the years, each one shaping her as she moved through her career. She began her journey as a personal assistant shortly after leaving school, stepping into a bustling office filled with an air of competitiveness and ambition. The environment at that time was harsh, heavily skewed towards male dominance, and it often felt like a battlefield where women had to prove their worth repeatedly. Yet, Lucy was not one to shy away from a challenge; she was a tenacious fighter with dreams that soared beyond the constraints of her surroundings.

Every morning, she would don her meticulously chosen outfits—smart blouses and pencil skirts—that spoke of the professionalism she embodied. As she entered the office, the scent of strong coffee and the chirping of pointless conversation filled the air. Long hours became the norm, and Lucy often pushed herself to go above and beyond, refusing to let the arduous nature of her work go unnoticed. In her mind, if her male colleagues offered one hundred percent, she would give two hundred percent, determined to carve out her own space in the corporate arena.

Her ambition fuelled her ascent, and it wasn't long before she climbed the ranks, from a general office manager to the esteemed Head of the HR department. This achievement was a testament to her dedication and hard work. In her new role, she thrived, surrounded by talented individuals who both challenged and inspired her. With each successful project, she relished the feeling of accomplishment.

However, after nearly a decade immersed in the same job, Lucy found herself awakening to a growing restlessness that whispered through the monotonous rhythm of her daily routine. Each morning, as she sipped her coffee, staring out at the street bustling with life, a wave of discontent washed over her. While she couldn't quite pinpoint what needed to shift, an insistent urge to break free from the familiar chains of her routine tugged at her heart.

One evening, after a long and heartfelt phone conversation with her brother Dale, a sense of clarity began to take shape. His encouraging words echoed in her mind, urging her to chase her dreams, igniting a spark of hope within her. Over the years, she had taken similar leaps of faith, each one leading her to unexpected joys and personal growth. Why not leap again? With each thought, the idea felt less daunting and more exhilarating.

Adding to her resolve was her best friend at work, Trisha, who had recently made the bold decision to leave behind her familiar life in pursuit of new adventures in Spain with her partner—a man she had met serendipitously on a sun-drenched holiday a couple of years earlier. Trisha's enthusiasm was contagious, a reminder that life was too short to remain stagnant. With Trisha's impending departure, Lucy sensed the timing was perfectly aligned for her own transformation.

As she mulled over her decision, the vibrant images of a life unbound danced in her mind. The thought of starting anew, of rediscovering herself beyond the confines of her desk, filled her with an intoxicating sense of possibility. "If I don't act now, when will I?" she asked herself, realising that the yearning for change had been simmering beneath the surface for far too long.

Trisha had asked Lucy to meet for coffee, eager to chat about her upcoming move to Spain and the whirlwind romance that had swept her off her feet nearly two years ago. The thought of starting a new chapter filled her with excitement, yet a tinge of sadness tugged at her heart—she dreaded leaving Lucy behind. Their bond had grown so strong over the past eight years that they had become almost like sisters, sharing countless moments and memories.

In the early days, Lucy had been the sole occupant of the HR department, managing everything with poise and dedication. But as the firm expanded, the decision was made to bring in a deputy head of HR—Trisha. Little did they know that this professional partnership would blossom into a deep-seated friendship that extended far beyond the confines of the office.

As Trisha settled at a charming outdoor café, the warmth of the midday sun wrapped around her like a cosy blanket. She felt its rays dancing on her skin, igniting a sense of contentment as she waited for Lucy. The table before her was adorned with steaming coffee cups, their rich aroma mingling with the faint scent of blooming flowers nearby. In her hands, she held a newspaper, her eyes occasionally drifting to scan the headlines, though her thoughts were preoccupied with her impending adventure.

Her short blonde hair glistened under the sunlight, sleek and stylish as it framed her face, with sunglasses perched jauntily atop her head. At fifty-three years old, Trisha possessed a striking beauty that many younger women envied, and the sun-kissed warmth of her complexion played up her captivating features, suggesting a life well-lived and filled with joy.

Trisha looked up from her crinkled newspaper, her eyes sparkling with delight as a huge smile spread across her face. With a swift motion, she folded the paper neatly, setting it down on the wooden table and leapt from her chair, arms outstretched in joyous anticipation. A burst of sunlight caught her friend Lucy, who was making her way across the car park, and Trisha couldn't help but beam at her approaching figure.

Lucy glanced over, her lips curling into a warm smile that could brighten even the dullest of days. Though her eyes were shielded behind stylish designer sunglasses, the happiness radiating from her was unmistakable. Her long, dark hair flowed down her back in gentle waves, catching the light and swaying gracefully with each step. Today, she'd chosen a casual yet eye-catching outfit that spoke of summer freedom; a pair of denim shorts that highlighted her legs and comfortably fitted trainers adorned with cheerful trainer socks. The pretty orange halter neck top draped effortlessly over her curves, accentuating her figure while complementing her sun-kissed skin.

Approaching her forties, Lucy often found herself mistaken for a much younger woman, likely due to her radiant skin and remarkable lack of wrinkles, a testament to her diligent skincare routine. But more than that, it was her youthful exuberance—a vibrant passion for life and a carefree sense of style that often leaned towards a relaxed, almost collegiate vibe—that contributed to the charming misconception.

Despite her confidence in many aspects of her life, Lucy grappled with a more profound struggle—the quiet, nagging shadow of self-doubt that often loomed over her. The scars from past relationships lingered in her heart, tangible reminders of painful experiences that had woven themselves into the fabric of her being. While friends frequently complimented her beauty, she found it nearly impossible to see herself through that lens.

As Lucy approached the table, a wave of anticipation washed over her, suddenly mixed with sadness. Trisha, animated as ever, threw her arms around her, and hugged her tightly, nearly lifting her off her feet. "Oh my god, I am going to miss this so much!" Trisha exclaimed; her voice laced with a bittersweet excitement. "What will we do when we can't just meet up for coffee and a chat anymore?" A hint of desperation hung in her tone.

"I don't know; I am going to feel lost without you," Lucy replied, her heart sinking as she spoke. Her brows furrowed in thought, and she added with a frown, "I already don't like this Peter they are bringing in to replace you, and I haven't even met him yet." The mention of a substitute felt like salt on an open wound.

Trisha chuckled lightly, trying to lighten the mood. "You never know; he could be the male version of me, and then you'd be just fine!" she laughed, but Lucy couldn't muster a smile. She paused for a moment, staring into Trisha's eyes that sparkled with mischief and warmth, before responding earnestly, "I cannot think of anything worse. Besides, there will only ever be one Trisha Pearce—male or female. You are one-of-a-kind, beautiful lady, and I am really going to miss you!"

As those words left her lips, Lucy felt a tear begin to form in the corner of her eye, betraying the composure she was struggling to maintain. In that moment, it struck her with heavy clarity: she was not just losing a colleague but a best friend, a confidante, someone who had enriched her life in countless ways.

It was not as if she could simply pop over for a quick visit or arrange to meet for their usual coffee beneath the sprawling oak tree in the park. Once her friend moved away, it would take a two-hour flight, a cumbersome journey that felt insurmountable in the face of their shared memories—the laughter, the late-night work marathons, the solace found in each other's company. The thought was overwhelming, a tidal wave of grief crashing through her.

The more Lucy contemplated the changes looming ahead, the more resentment bubbled inside her, directed not just at the impending void in her life but at the very office that would now feel empty without Trisha's vibrant spirit. All those days spent dreaming of new opportunities began to surface in her mind, whispering promises of adventure and excitement—what if now, in this moment of poignant change, was her chance to finally pursue them?

Lucy and Trisha spent the next couple of hours wrapped in animated conversation, their voices occasionally rising with excitement as they discussed Trisha's new life under the warm Spanish sun, living alongside the man of her dreams. The cosy café, filled with the rich aroma of freshly brewed coffee and the soft murmur of other customers, served as the perfect backdrop for their plans. They sketched out a vibrant itinerary of regular trips, envisioning weekends filled with laughter and adventure, where Lucy could bask in the golden rays of Spain's shores and perhaps catch the eye of charming locals. They envisioned leisurely afternoons on the beach and intimate evenings filled with the thrill of new romance.

Although Lucy found herself currently in a relationship, a sense of unease gnawed at her. She recognised deep down that it wasn't truly fulfilling, and she grappled with the understanding that her life was in dire need of change if she ever wanted to embrace genuine happiness. This realisation sparked within her a flame of determination, urging her to act. With newfound resolve coursing through her veins, Lucy decided that her first step towards transformation would be to resign from her job and embark on a fresh career path.

As they finished their steaming mugs of coffee, a bittersweet feeling enveloped them. The two friends stood, their arms wrapping around each other in a warm embrace, savouring the moment that would soon become a cherished memory. Trisha's impending departure hung heavy in the air, and Lucy felt a mix of dread and admiration for her friend's brave new beginning. They had promised each other that on Monday, Lucy would walk into her workplace and hand in her notice—a pivotal moment etched in their minds.

As Lucy navigated the familiar streets leading home, her mind raced with thoughts about the conversation she was about to have with her partner, Johnathon. She was confident that he would ultimately support her decision to resign, yet she knew she needed to express her reasons clearly and thoughtfully.

As she neared their small, two-story house, doubt crept in, clouding her resolve. A twinge of anxiety made her consider circling the estate for a little while longer, giving herself just a few more moments to gather her thoughts. However, as she caught sight of Johnathon's car parked in the driveway, reality hit her: he was already home, and the time for conversation was now. Taking a deep breath to steady herself, Lucy pulled into her space and stepped out, her determination renewed.

The soft crunch of gravel beneath her feet accompanied her as she walked towards the front door, her heart pounding. Just as she reached for the handle, the door swung open with an abruptness that startled her. There, stood Johnathon, a tall figure with a slightly plump build, his unkempt beard and messy short hair giving him a frazzled appearance. His brow was furrowed in concern, and his eyes darted impatiently.

"Where have you been?" he exclaimed, his voice rising with urgency. "I've had some problems with the car, and I need you to take me somewhere. I need to pick something up right now! When I tried to use my own car, it wouldn't start. I don't know what's wrong with it, but I can't wait!"

Lucy felt a cold wave wash over her as she processed his words. He seemed completely oblivious to her own turmoil, wrapped up in his own needs and demands. For him, it was as if her feelings didn't register at all. She stood there, expressionless, feeling as though she were a shadow in her own life.

"I need to talk to you about something important," Lucy said, her voice steady despite the turmoil inside.

"That's fine; we can talk on the way!" Johnathon responded without missing a beat, snatching her keys from her hand with a sense of urgency that left her momentarily speechless. He headed towards her car, each step echoing her growing frustration. Reluctantly, Lucy followed, her heart sinking as she realised their long-overdue conversation was being swept aside yet again. Hope flickered within her that perhaps, just perhaps, they could have that crucial discussion on the journey—if only he would let her speak.

As they drove along the winding road, the late afternoon sun cast a warm glow through the car windows, illuminating the dust notes dancing in the air. Johnathon animatedly talked about a crucial piece of equipment he needed for his computer, his voice rising and falling with enthusiasm. Yet, Lucy found herself drifting away from his words, her mind wandering into daydreams of a new career — one that she could step into with confidence. The thought of embracing a fresh start both excited and daunted her. Time was running out; she had not yet discovered that new path and needed to act fast if she was going to hand in her notice on Monday—just two short days away. With a determined flicker in her eyes, she resolved that this weekend would be dedicated to unearthing her new career, regardless of whether Johnathon supported her decision.

"Are you even listening to me?" Johnathon's voice sliced through her reverie, filled with a mixture of annoyance and exasperation. Lucy glanced over at him, her eyes wide with surprise, and responded with a touch of irritation, "Like you have been listening to me? I clearly told you back at the house that I needed to talk to you about something important! And all you've done is ramble on about your bloody computer! Honestly, I care about your computer as much as you care about me!"

The words hung heavy in the space between them as Johnathon sat in stunned silence, his gaze fixed on Lucy as she steered the car. The tension in the air was palpable. He was taken aback, realising that whatever Lucy wanted to discuss was far more significant than he had initially understood. Thoughts swirled in his mind; he had thought they were both coping with Trisha's departure, but now he grasped the depth of Lucy's emotions. The glimmer of determination in her eyes told him that this was more than just a fleeting thought. Something pivotal was at stake, and he felt a gnawing sense of worry begin to stir within him.

"Is it because Trisha is going?" Johnathon asked, his brow furrowing with concern as he glanced over at Lucy, who was staring blankly out of the car windscreen at the road ahead of them.

"No!" Lucy replied sharply, her voice cutting through the silence like a knife. The warmth of the afternoon sun contrasted with the chill that had entered her tone.

"Then what is it?" he pressed, still trying to decipher the tension that hung thickly in the air between them.

"I need to change my life," she finally said, turning to face him with a fire in her eyes. "I am not happy! Something has to change." Her heart raced with the weight of her revelation, each word a declaration of her intent.

"What do you need to change to make you happy?" he inquired, his voice tinged with a mix of confusion and worry.

"I'm going to hand in my notice at work on Monday!" she declared, a sense of determination lacing her words. There was a flicker of hope in her chest, a yearning for something more than the monotony of her daily routine.

"WHAT?" he yelled in disbelief, his voice echoing against the car's interior. "You cannot just quit your job! What are you going to do? We both need to work to maintain our lifestyle. If you quit, how will we pay the bills and afford the things we enjoy? No, I don't think you should do that," Johnathon insisted, his tone bordering on frantic.

"I will do what I want, Johnathon," Lucy retorted, her voice unwavering but cracking under the strain of her emotions. "It's my decision to make, not yours! I am going to submit my notice on Monday, whether you like it or not." The conviction in her words was like a shield, guarding her inner turmoil. "Oh, and by the way, I haven't found another job yet, but I guarantee I will have one by the time my notice period is up! I am not asking for your opinion or your permission. I was looking for some support, and I didn't get it, so there you have it."

Lucy's frustration boiled over, and she turned back to the windscreen, the vibrant landscape blurring in her peripheral vision. The air between them was thick with unspoken words and unresolved feelings, and she felt a deep, simmering anger that rendered her speechless for the rest of the trip.

As soon as Lucy stepped into her house, a familiar air of determination enveloped her. With her laptop perched open in front of her, she dove headfirst into a sea of job sites, her fingers dancing over the keyboard in a rhythmic search for opportunities. One particular listing caught her eye—a position working with young offenders. The thought initially felt daunting; Lucy had never considered herself much of a "people person." However, beneath her reserved exterior lay a resilience that allowed her to mimic the social ease she often envied in others.

Her heart raced with both apprehension and excitement as she pondered the nature of the work. It was outside her comfort zone, but it also felt refreshingly intriguing. "What do I have to lose?" she mused, her thoughts spiralling into a hopeful future as she carefully crafted her application. After polishing her CV and creating a cover letter that reflected both her skills and her willingness to adapt, she hit 'send' with a deep breath, the weight of uncertainty now mingling with a taste of possibility.

About a week later, while seated at her desk with the afternoon sun streaming through the window, an unexpected email notification flashed across her screen. She squinted at the subject line, momentarily dismissing it as just another invite for a HR job. A familiar sense of reluctance washed over her, and she hesitated to click it open—was it worth getting her hopes up? Deciding to wait until she returned home from work, she tucked the thought away, aware that time was not on her side. With a resolve that came from necessity, she reminded herself that she couldn't retract her resignation, despite her boss's desperate pleas for her to stay.

Throughout the day, the email kept surfacing in her mind, an irksome whisper tugging at her thoughts. Finally, after what felt like an eternity of indecision, she resolved to open it. As she read through the carefully composed lines, the words leapt out at her with burgeoning excitement:

Dear Lucy,

We would like to formally invite you to an interview for the position of Youth Offending Worker at Dale House, Worthington, on the 2nd of August at 10 AM.

Lucy couldn't believe her eyes. A rush of disbelief surged through her, mixed with elation; this was the one job she had been yearning for, the role she had convinced herself was beyond her reach. An invitation to interview felt almost surreal, a golden opportunity she had dared to dream about but never fully expected.

In the days that followed, anticipation morphed into determination as Lucy immersed herself in research about Dale House. She wandered through the website, absorbing every detail like a sponge and capturing the essence of the organisation's mission. She meticulously compiled a binder brimming with notes, crammed with examples from her past experiences that would serve as the foundation for the evidence-based questions she anticipated encountering during the interview.

Understanding the gravity of her aspirations, Lucy was laser-focused on enhancing her knowledge of youth offending. She delved deep into the statistics that painted a troubling picture, exploring the patterns of offending and reoffending with fervour. Page after page, she uncovered the myriad of reasons behind these distressing behaviours, from socioeconomic factors to familial influences, all while gathering an array of related information that could lend depth to her discussions.

As the days ticked by, she felt the weight of the impending interview settle upon her shoulders. Lucy was resolute; she would not let this opportunity slip through her fingers. With each passing moment, her excitement was fuelled by the promise of making a difference in the lives of young people, a chance to contribute to something greater than herself.

As she prepared, Lucy felt a growing sense of confidence and excitement. She couldn't wait to step into the interview room, armed with knowledge and insights, ready to impress her interviewers and display her dedication. Earlier that week, she had tried to share her excitement with Johnathon, hoping for his support. However, his reaction was far from enthusiastic; he was visibly displeased, primarily because the salary for the new position was considerably lower than her current job. Lucy tried to explain her perspective, emphasising how the negative atmosphere of her current job was weighing heavily on her. Yet, Johnathon remained unconvinced, asserting that she shouldn't abandon everything she had known for the past decade simply because she was feeling unfulfilled.

⊶⊷⟨⟩⊶⊷

Chapter Two

It felt like an eternity for Lucy as she sat in her small, sunlit home, anxiously awaiting the moment of her long-anticipated interview. The walls were adorned with motivational quotes that she had collected over the years, a silent testament to her determination and resilience. She meticulously prepared for this opportunity, pouring over her CV and researching every aspect of the company, determined to present herself in the best possible light.

Each night, as the locals around her estate buzzed with the sounds of fun and laughter, she practiced her responses to potential questions in front of the mirror, striving to perfect her confidence and poise. The weight of her decision hung heavily on her shoulders; she had turned down several other interviews for HR positions that never truly resonated with her heart or aspirations. Those roles felt like dead ends, and despite the nagging fear of delaying her career further, she held firm in her conviction that this job was what she truly desired.

Now, as the clock ticked closer to the interview time, a sense of urgency and anxiety surged within her. The thought of not securing this position loomed large in her mind, especially with her current job's departure date rapidly approaching. If she failed to impress, it would mean scrambling to find something else in an increasingly competitive landscape—a challenge she worried she might not be ready to face.

Moreover, Johnathon's voice echoed in her head, casting a shadow of doubt over her ambitions. He had warned her against taking such a leap back to the bottom of the career ladder, calling her decisions reckless. But Lucy was unwavering in her belief that success isn't solely marked by title or position and that this particular opportunity could be the springboard she needed to fulfil her true potential. She took a deep breath, steeling herself for the moment that would define her next steps.

Lucy sat in the waiting room at Dale House, her heart racing as she awaited her interview. The air was thick with anticipation, and she could feel a mixture of nerves and excitement swirling within her. She took a deep breath, reminding herself that if she just held her nerve, she had a real chance of landing this job.

Dressed in a tailored navy suit that complemented her figure, she had made a conscious effort to present herself impeccably. Unlike her usual habit of arriving slightly late, today she had ensured she arrived twenty minutes early, her desire to make a commendable first impression burning bright. The walls of the waiting room were painted in soft, calming shades of beige, adorned with abstract artwork that added a touch of sophistication.

As she stared at the clock on the wall, its hands moved slowly, each tick echoing in the stillness of the room. The chime of 10 a.m. rang out, sharp and clear, slicing through her thoughts. Suddenly, a door at the far end of the room creaked open. A friendly-looking woman emerged, her shoulder-length blonde curls bouncing lightly with her movements. Her warm smile illuminated the space, dispelling some of Lucy's anxiety.

"Lucy?" she called, her voice inviting and cheerful. "Come on in."

Lucy's heart fluttered as she got to her feet, trying to project an air of confidence despite the whirlwind of emotions inside her. As she stepped forward, the door closed behind her with a soft thud, sealing away the waiting room and ushering her into the unknown—where the magic of possibility awaited.

As Lucy stepped out of the interview room, she let out a deep sigh of relief, the tension that had been coiling in her chest finally beginning to ease. The polished wooden door closed behind her with a soft click, and she paused for a moment, letting the ambient sounds of the bustling office wash over her. The thrill of completing the interview pulsed through her veins, mingled with a flutter of anxiety about the outcome.

The panel had patiently explained their timeline, assuring her that she would hear back from them by Friday—just three days away. That seemed both an eternity and a heartbeat away. Lucy glanced back at the door, her heart racing as she recalled the questions they had posed and how she had navigated each one with a blend of confidence and vulnerability.

With a gracious smile, she had thanked the three interviewers for their time, feeling the warmth of their firm handshakes as she exchanged pleasantries. Each handshake felt like a small anchor in that moment, grounding her as she processed the experience. Stepping away from the panel, she held her head high, the weight of self-doubt lifting with each stride. The corridor stretched ahead, bright and inviting, a path leading her toward what lay next in her journey.

Lucy stepped outside, where the warm sunlight enveloped her like a comforting embrace. She paused for a moment, allowing the gentle breeze to tousle her hair as she contemplated the outcome of her interview. The three-day wait for news loomed over her like a dark cloud, but she reminded herself that at least it wasn't a week or longer. With a deep breath, she climbed into her car, the familiar scent of vanilla air freshener filling her nostrils and cranked up the volume on her favourite playlist. The pulsating beats reverberated in her chest as she pulled out onto the open road, her worries dancing away with the rhythm of the music.

As she drove closer to home, a wave of excitement mixed with apprehension washed over her. She had been eager to share the news with Johnathon, yet a nagging doubt crept in—would he truly be supportive, or would he find a way to dim her enthusiasm with his sceptical remarks? Shaking off the thought, Lucy turned into the gravel driveway, the crunching sound beneath her tires echoing in the stillness of the late afternoon. She switched off the engine and stepped out, the sun casting a golden hue on everything around her.

Just as she opened the driver's door, her phone buzzed insistently in her handbag, causing her heart to race. Digging through the clutter of her bag, she felt a surge of anxiety as she nearly missed the call.

The caller ID flashed: Dale House. A sinking feeling settled in her stomach—this had to be unwelcome news.

"Hello?" she answered hesitantly, her voice a mix of hope and dread.

"Hello there, is that Lucy DeMarco?" the voice on the other end chimed, smooth and reassuring.

"It is, yes," Lucy replied, her pulse quickening.

"Hello again, Lucy, it's Bridget from the interview you attended today at Dale House. I need to tell you that my colleagues and I were extremely impressed with you and have made the collective decision to offer you the job!"

For a moment, silence enveloped Lucy as disbelief washed over her. Was this truly happening? She felt a rush of exhilaration, a flood of joy bursting forth after what felt like ages of uncertainty and longing.

"Lucy?" Bridget prompted gently, breaking the magical spell of silence. "Will you be accepting the role?"

"Oh, my goodness, yes! Yes, yes, yes!" Lucy exclaimed, her voice bubbling over with excitement. "Thank you so much for this opportunity; I promise I will not let you down!"

"We know!" Bridget responded with enthusiasm. "I will get our HR department to prepare everything to get you started as soon as possible, if you're happy with that?"

"Oh, yes, absolutely! I honestly cannot wait!" Lucy cried, her heart soaring, each beat amplifying her excitement for what lay ahead. In that moment, the uncertainties of the past melted away, replaced by boundless possibilities.

As Lucy stepped through the polished glass doors of the office, a rush of excitement mingled with a wave of anxiety washed over her. The bright, open space buzzed with the energy of her new colleagues, laughter and conversation weaving through the air like vibrant threads. She noticed clusters of coworkers huddled together, engaging in animated discussions, and a pang of unease tightened in her stomach.

Just a week earlier, those same faces had been strangers, joining the team alongside her fellow newcomers, while Lucy had been tethered to her old job by a lengthy notice period. The memories of her old office loomed in her mind, a reminder of how long she had dedicated her life to a place that was now behind her, both a comfort and a weight.

The unfamiliar surroundings heightened her apprehension; she had never been particularly adept at forming friendships. The fact that she was the latecomer only deepened her sense of isolation, as if an invisible barrier had been erected between her and the others. It felt like stepping onto a stage where everyone else already knew their lines. Yet, despite the trepidation fluttering in her chest, Lucy held her head high, squared her shoulders, and took a deep breath. With determination coursing through her, she stepped further into the space, ready to face whatever awaited her in this new chapter of her life.

As Lucy stepped into the office, she was met by her manager, Tom, who greeted her with a curt nod and gestured for her to follow him inside. The atmosphere was a blend of anticipation and unease, the air thick with the scent of polished wood and the faint aroma of coffee. Tom was an older gentleman, impeccably dressed in a tailored suit that accentuated his overweight figure. His grey hair was neatly combed back, and the glasses perched on his nose framed his sharp, discerning eyes.

At first, Tom's demeanour felt reminiscent of a stern headteacher; he introduced himself with an expression that suggested neither warmth nor welcome. Lucy couldn't shake the feeling that she had somehow already disappointed him, perhaps for not being able to start the week earlier as discussed. Surely, that couldn't be the reason for his serious countenance, but doubt crept into her mind.

As he began to distribute thick booklets and worksheets, his voice was steady and authoritative, yet devoid of any conversational warmth. Each paper landed in front of Lucy like an assignment rather than a welcome pack, and the quiet rustle of the materials seemed to echo in the tense silence between them. Lucy shifted in her seat, the chair feeling too large, and the sensation of being on display only amplified her discomfort. With each passing moment, she felt the pressure of breaking the ice growing heavier, anxiously contemplating what would be the right words to ease the tension that hung in the room. As Lucy adjusted her posture, preparing to unleash a light-hearted joke to ease the atmosphere, the door swung open. In walked a younger man with an easy smile that lit up his face, instantly brightening the room. "Did you ask for me, Tom?" he said, his voice warm and inviting.

"I did," Tom replied, his tone both professional and encouraging. "I'd like you to take Lucy here out with you today to meet your clients. She needs to shadow for a few days, so I've aligned her shifts with yours to help her learn the ropes of how we operate around here."

"Sure thing, Tom. No problem at all," Liam responded with a nod, exuding confidence, and friendliness. He turned his attention to Lucy, his smile growing wider as he extended his hand toward her. "Hi, I'm Liam. Nice to meet you. Shall we go?"

As Lucy reached out to shake his hand, she felt a spark of excitement mixed with a tinge of nerves. His grip was firm yet gentle, and his eyes conveyed a sense of approachability that instantly eased her apprehensions. She eagerly accepted the opportunity, her mind racing with thoughts of the day ahead. This marked the beginning of a new life for Lucy, and she felt both excited and prepared for it.

Time seemed to spiral swiftly at Dale House, an institution bustling with energy and purpose. Lucy couldn't believe how quickly three months had flown by since she first walked through its welcoming doors. The excitement she felt was palpable as she recalled taking on her own list of clients just three weeks into her role, diving headfirst into the responsibilities that came with her position. She was flourishing, her enthusiasm translating into tangible results that earned her the admiration of those around her.

The youths she worked with warmed to her effortlessly; they found comfort in her presence. Colleagues often described Lucy as sweet and light-hearted, yet she maintained an admirable firmness that radiated fairness. Each morning, as the sun peeked through her curtains, she leaped out of bed with a sense of purpose, eager to embrace the day ahead. There was no temptation to pull the duvet back, seeking solace under its cosy weight, nor any fleeting thoughts of concocting excuses to take a day off or to work from the confines of her home.

At Dale House, Lucy had truly found her footing amidst the variety of personalities and interactions. While she navigated the complexities of workplace dynamics, naturally, she encountered individuals with whom she didn't quite click. However, it was her small circle of close colleagues that brought her joy—their shared laughter and camaraderie transformed even the longest days into moments that vanished swiftly in the backdrop of collaboration and support. Each hour spent together turned the routine into a delightful dance of productivity, making time at Dale House feel like a rewarding journey rather than just a job.

As time drifted on, Lucy found herself enveloped in a growing sense of longing. It was as if a vibrant flame of ambition had been ignited within her, revealing she had so much more to offer the world. She couldn't shake the feeling of being left behind, especially as she watched close colleagues, once a part of her daily routine, embrace new opportunities at different companies. Each farewell echoed in her mind, fuelling her desire to seek out a slice of that excitement for herself.

The nostalgia for her former friend Trisha hit her like a wave; it felt like an eternity since they had shared a laugh or a cup of coffee. Lucy missed those moments deeply, yet her new friends at Dale House had developed a support network that made the sting of Trisha's absence easier to bear—almost as if they had created a comforting cocoon around her. Almost, but not quite, for Trisha's laughter still rang in her ears sometimes, and it was a reminder of her longing for deeper connections.

However, Lucy felt a heavy cloud of isolation settle over her when she considered discussing her aspirations with Johnathon. After his dismissive reaction to her previous job inquiries, she knew that bringing it up again would only deepen her sense of solitude. Each day, her family remained oblivious to her internal struggles, their lack of interest echoing her own feelings of despair. Friends, caught up in the whirlwind of their own busy lives, seemed to have little time to offer her the guidance she desperately sought.

The following day, Lucy arrived at work, her heart a mix of excitement and trepidation. She had a shift lined up with Liam, her colleague, who was also on the brink of change, ready to leap towards a new company soon. As they settled into the rhythm of their tasks, Lucy mustered the courage to ask Liam about the new company and why so many of their team were embarking on different paths.

Liam leaned in closer, his eyes sparkling with enthusiasm as he explained the opportunities waiting beyond their current role. He spoke of career progression possibilities that seemed to burst with potential, descriptions of environments buzzing with innovation and support, and the allure of personal growth that seemed just within reach. With every word, Lucy felt her own dreams take flight in her mind, igniting a flicker of hope that perhaps it wasn't too late for her to chase what she truly desired. "I think I need to take that leap too, but I don't know if I'm ready to!" Lucy exclaimed, her voice tinged with uncertainty as she fiddled with the edge of her notebook, the pages slightly worn from countless scribbles and notes. Liam, sitting across from her, leaned forward with an encouraging smile, his wide eyes sparkling with enthusiasm. "Are you kidding? Of course you are," he replied with genuine conviction, his voice full of warmth. "You're one of the most talented youth offending workers at our office. Seriously, any other company would be thrilled to have someone with your skills and passion."

He paused for a moment, glancing out the window at the bustling street below, before continuing with a sense of urgency in his tone. "If you're serious about making a change, I can give you a name and an email address to contact for an interview. They're hiring right now, and it's actually the place I'm planning to go myself," he added, his excitement contagious.

Lucy's heart raced at the thought of new possibilities. She took a deep breath, her resolve slowly hardening. "Okay, yeah, why not," she said, a hint of determination creeping into her voice. "I guess it can't hurt to try, can it?" A flicker of hope sparked in her eyes as she considered the chance for growth just within her grasp.

Chapter Three

All of Lucy's favourite colleagues had moved on now, leaving a profound emptiness in the bustling office environment. The laughter and camaraderie that once filled the air had faded, replaced by an unsettling silence that echoed around her. She felt flat and low, her spirits sinking deeper with each passing day, and she found herself desperately missing Trisha, her confidante and friend.

When she received the email from the company Liam had encouraged her to contact, her heart sank. The message was brief and cold, only offering the disappointing news that they weren't currently recruiting but would reach out as soon as opportunities arose. Devastation washed over Lucy, a heavy tide of disappointment that threatened to pull her under.

The office now felt alien to her; it was populated with unfamiliar faces who seemed to have formed an instant connection, laughing, and chatting as if they'd known each other for years. Lucy, once a vibrant part of the dynamic team, now felt like an outsider looking in. She had transitioned into the role of the mother figure, offering advice and support, but it was a stark contrast to the fun-loving peer she had been just a couple of months earlier.

As Lucy stepped out of the dimly lit office, the cool evening air wrapped around her like a refreshing blanket after a long day. She reached into her handbag, her fingers searching through the layers of clutter for her car keys, which seemed to have vanished among the jumble of lipsticks, notes, and tissues. Just as her frustration was beginning to mount, her mobile phone chimed, piercing the quiet of the carpark and breaking her concentration.

Curiosity piqued, Lucy pulled her phone from its cosy spot and instinctively swiped down on the screen to check the email notification that had just arrived. As her eyes skimmed the sender's address, a jolt of intrigue coursed through her—was it really them? She had reached out to this company a couple of months earlier after Liam had given her the contact details, only to receive a polite yet firm response indicating that they weren't currently hiring.

Confusion settled in as she opened the email, her heart racing slightly. The message unfurled before her eyes, inviting her to come in for a meeting, the words a stark contrast to the previous rejection. Why would they reach out now? The warmth of the setting sun washed over her, but Lucy felt a chill of uncertainty. The evening had just taken an unexpected turn, and she couldn't shake the feeling that this could be a pivotal moment for her career.

Excitement surged through Lucy's veins like an electric current as she meticulously prepared for her meeting with the new potential employer. The air was thick with anticipation; they had neither confirmed nor denied the possibility of a job offer when she had phoned, instead casually mentioning their desire to meet to explore future opportunities within their organisation.

As Lucy sat in the sleek, modern waiting area, her heart raced with the thrill of what might lie ahead. She had dressed to impress, choosing a fitted blazer that accentuated her silhouette and tailored trousers that exuded professionalism.

Every detail of her appearance conveyed a sense of readiness and ambition, as she envisioned not just a job, but a new chapter in her career. Lucy took a deep breath, her pulse steadying as she reminded herself of the skills and experiences she brought to the table, eager to display her potential to the team that awaited her. Lucy scanned the room and saw a young woman heading towards her. This is it; she thought. This must be who the meeting is with, Lucy thought as she observed the woman glide toward her, her movements confident and commanding. The woman's smile was warm yet fleeting, almost like a whisper of acknowledgment, before she elegantly sashayed past Lucy and into the bright embrace of the Spring air outside. Lucy felt a spiral of uncertainty, concluding that perhaps this wasn't the person she was meant to meet after all.

As she sat in the waiting area, time seemed to stretch into eternity, the soft hum of distant conversations and the rustling of papers around her both calming and disorienting. Just when Lucy began to wonder if she might be overlooked entirely, her name pierced through the ambient noise: "Lucy DeMarco?!"

Startled, she stood abruptly, her heart racing as she focused on the older gentleman who stood in front of her. His shirt was an unusual sight—half tucked in, half spilling out in a careless manner, reflecting a hasty wardrobe choice. His hair was tousled, giving him the appearance of someone who had just rushed in from an intense downpour rather than a professional meeting. A suspicious stain marred his trousers, a dark smudge that told tales of hurried meals and chaotic mornings.

Not exactly the polished professional she had anticipated, Lucy thought, but she reminded herself that appearances could be deceiving. Mustering her composure, she extended her arm, a smile gracing her lips. "Hello, I'm Lucy," she introduced herself, hoping to bridge the gap between their first impressions.

The man, engrossed in chewing something audibly with his mouth open, paused mid-bite upon seeing her extend her hand. After a beat of hesitation, he lifted his hand only to hesitate again, deciding to wipe it on his trousers, leaving a faint residue before finally offering it to her for a handshake. Lucy's smile faltered ever so slightly, but she kept her demeanour composed, ready to embrace whatever this meeting might bring.

The meeting felt remarkably casual, resembling a friendly catch-up rather than a formal job interview. With animated gestures and an infectious enthusiasm, she delved into the details of her experiences at Dale House. Despite having been in her role for only a fleeting period, she exuded confidence as she highlighted her achievements, painting a vibrant picture of her contributions as a youth offending worker.

Lucy spoke passionately about the various initiatives she had spearheaded, illustrating how she had quickly adapted to the demands of her position. With each success story, she wove a narrative of growth and resilience, highlighting her ability to thrive even in challenging situations. Her rapid ascent to training inexperienced staff was both a point of pride and a source of initial trepidation for her. She vividly recalled the mix of excitement and fear she felt at the prospect of guiding others before fully finding her footing in the role. Yet, as she navigated those early days, Lucy discovered a profound understanding of her responsibilities, transforming her self-doubt into a compelling conviction.

Phil, who had been listening intently, leaned forward with an air of curiosity and admiration. Halfway through the conversation, he introduced himself with a firm handshake and genuine interest. His questions were thoughtful, reflecting his engagement in Lucy's narrative. "Did you bring a copy of your CV with you for me to have a look at?" he inquired, his eyes sparkling with anticipation. Lucy's heart swelled with confidence as she handed over her meticulously organised CV, proud of the achievements it encapsulated. Phil perused the CV intently, the faint rustle of paper punctuating the otherwise quiet room. After a few minutes, he looked up, peering over the rim of his glasses. A subtle, almost enigmatic smile danced at the corners of his lips as he set the CV down on the polished wooden surface before him. With a deliberate motion, he removed his glasses and placed them gently beside the document.

Across from him, Lucy sat poised in a plush armchair, its fabric a deep shade of navy that contrasted with the soft beige of the room. She could feel the weight of his gaze, an almost tangible force that made her shift uncomfortably in her seat. The small table that separated them seemed to amplify the tension, a barrier yet to be crossed. After a brief moment, Phil let out a soft, contented sigh, a sound that seemed to fill the space between them. He rose to his feet with an air of relaxed confidence, his presence commanding yet inviting. Lucy instinctively followed suit, her heart quickening in apprehension.

"Well, young lady," he began, his voice warm and reassuring, "Welcome to the team. When can you start?" The words hung in the air, a blend of opportunity and anticipation that made the room feel charged with possibility.

Lucy began her new role at Tates & Co two weeks later, filled with a mix of excitement and apprehension. To her relief, several familiar faces from her days at Dale House were also employed at Tates & Co. Their presence wrapped her in a comforting sense of camaraderie, dissolving the feelings of isolation she'd experienced in her previous role amongst the new team. No longer was she relegated to the title of "mum" in her professional life; instead, she felt a renewed sense of belonging.

As the days unfolded, time seemed to accelerate at Tates & Co, a stark contrast to the languid pace she had grown accustomed to at Dale House. Lucy thrived in this vibrant environment; her skill set blossoming as she embraced the challenges of her role. Recognition soon followed; she earned Employee of the Month awards, accompanied by attractive vouchers that her colleagues presented with enthusiastic applause. Yet, she remained humble, attributing her success to teamwork and the supportive atmosphere that surrounded her.

In a mere six months, Lucy had not only adapted but flourished, gaining countless new qualifications and accolades. Each achievement marked her ascent in the company, signifying her dedication and hard work. With every passing day, she felt more at home, solidifying her place at Tates & Co. At last, Lucy had not just found her job; she had discovered her true calling, thriving in the rhythm of her new life, and embracing the sense of purpose it brought her.

One crisp, sunlit morning, with a hint of frost still lingering in the air, Lucy made her way to the office, a buoyant anticipation coursing through her veins. It was just another day, yet every morning felt like a fresh start, brimming with promise. As she stepped into the bustling atmosphere of Tates and Co, the familiar scent of coffee and the soft sound of chatter welcomed her. The vibrant energy of her workplace was invigorating, a clear sign that she had found genuine job satisfaction.

Pushing open the office door, Lucy was immediately greeted by the lively buzz of her colleagues. She noticed Liam, Kate, and Josh huddled in a tight circle near the coffee machine, their expressions tinged with excitement and secrecy as they whispered among themselves. Curious, she removed her puffy, winter coat, carefully hanging it on the coat stand, and then made her way towards the kitchen area.

Kate, a petite woman with a cascade of glossy blonde hair that framed her face, stood out with her dramatic makeup and form-fitting suit that left little to the imagination. She flashed Lucy an exaggerated grin, her huge eyelashes fluttering as she exclaimed, "They're bringing people up from the London office to spy on us!"

Taken aback, Lucy raised an eyebrow and asked, "What? For what reason?" Her mind raced with possibilities—was there trouble brewing within their ranks?

Liam, his brow furrowed, and arms crossed, chimed in with a mix of concern and intrigue, "We don't really know. We overheard management discussing it, and they said something about needing to keep an eye on some of us. Apparently, the London team will be inconspicuously blending in here for a few weeks." His voice dropped to a conspiratorial whisper, making the atmosphere even more charged with tension.

Lucy's head swirled with thoughts, wondering what this unexpected visit might mean for their close-knit team. She felt a blend of excitement and apprehension. What changes lay ahead?

Mid-afternoon sunlight streamed through the tall windows of Phil's office, casting a warm glow on the polished wooden desk between him and Lucy. As Lucy entered, Phil gestured to a plush chair opposite him, his tone cordial yet authoritative. She settled into the chair, smoothing her skirt before folding her hands in her lap. Phil had a habit of clicking his pens incessantly when he sat at his desk—a rhythmic staccato that drummed into Lucy's ears and tested her patience. Despite the annoyance bubbling within her, she forced herself to maintain a calm exterior, focusing on the patterns of light dancing across the carpet rather than the nagging sound.

"So, Lucy, as I'm sure you have probably heard from the gossip stations," he began, leaning forward slightly, his expression a mix of excitement and seriousness, "We have some colleagues joining us from London for a few weeks." His voice held an air of authority as he continued, "They will be accompanying you all to meet clients individually. They're here to lend a hand and assess the growth and development of the business, so there's really nothing to worry about."

Lucy maintained her composure, though a knot formed in her stomach at the thought of outsiders evaluating her work. "Anyway," Phil went on, a smile spreading across his face, "I have assigned Jack Archer to you. He'll be working with you day-to-day for the next few weeks."

At the mention of Jack's name, Lucy's mind raced. Who was this new colleague? Would he be helpful, or would he just complicate her routine? Phil continued, "Please make him feel welcome and comfortable, and carry on doing exactly what you do!" His enthusiasm was palpable, but Lucy felt a flicker of resistance rising inside her.

She hesitated, weighing the desire to voice her concerns against the need to keep the peace with her manager. Ultimately, she chose silence for now, her curiosity piqued about what Monday would bring. As the conversation wound down, she couldn't shake the feeling that change was on the horizon, and she had only a fleeting glimpse of what was to come.

When Lucy finally stepped through the door of her house after a long day at work, she felt a familiar twinge of guilt wash over her. It was time to reach out to Trisha, her best friend whom she had nearly neglected over the past few months. With a deep breath, she picked up her phone and pressed on Trisha's name, an act that felt both necessary and overdue.

As the phone rang, Lucy couldn't shake the wave of nostalgia that hit her—memories of laughter-filled nights and shared dreams flooded her mind. She recalled the ambitious plans they had made, envisioning Lucy's journey to Spain to meet the man of her dreams, all while rekindling the bond that had made them inseparable. But now, the distance felt palpable, and a hint of sadness settled in her chest as the call transitioned to voicemail.

Just as she prepared to leave a message, her phone buzzed with an incoming call. Her heart raced with a mixture of hope and excitement—it was Trisha calling back. "Oh my god, I have missed your voice so much!" Lucy exclaimed, a smile spreading across her face as she answered the call. "Same!" Trisha replied, her enthusiasm echoing through the line.

For the next two hours, the conversation flowed effortlessly, like a refreshing stream through a parched desert. Trisha shared vibrant stories of her adventures in Spain—the bustling market streets filled with vibrant fruits, the sun-kissed beaches where she had lounged effortlessly baking, and the charming little café where she indulged in rich, velvety chocolate on churros. As she recounted her new job as an English teacher in a lively Spanish school, Lucy could practically hear the enthusiasm in her friend's voice. Trisha had always excelled in languages, effortlessly weaving her words with a melodic flair.

Then, the conversation took an intriguing turn as they delved into the enigmatic world of Jack Archer—the international super spy whose adventures seemed to leap off the pages of a thrilling novel. They swapped theories, laughed at outlandish spy antics, and filled the air with their shared excitement, the bond between them rekindled as brightly as ever. In that moment, all the distance and time melted away, replaced by a warmth that only true friendship could ignite. With a lingering sense of anticipation, Lucy ended the call, the faint echo of the conversation still dancing in her mind. The promise of an update about the elusive Jack Archer hung in the air like the sweet scent of spring blossoms. She felt a mix of excitement and anxiety as she climbed the creaking staircase to her bedroom. As she nestled beneath her warm quilt her thoughts began to drift. With a sigh, she closed her eyes, surrendering to the possibilities that awaited her in the coming days.

Chapter Four

Monday dawned with a crispness in the air that seemed to energise Lucy in ways she hadn't anticipated. As she walked into the office, her heels clicked assertively against the polished floor, echoing her confidence. There was a noticeable spring in her step, fuelled not just by her eagerness to dive into the day's tasks, but by a newfound sense of determination.

Lucy felt a surge of arrogance coursing through her veins—a feeling that was both empowering and mildly unsettling. Over the weekend, thoughts of Jack Archer had consumed her mind, and she had made a resolute decision: it was time to show him exactly with whom he was dealing. She imagined herself standing before him, unwavering and firm, her eyes locking onto his with a blaze of conviction. She was not just a fiercely strong woman; she was a force to be reckoned with, unafraid to voice her thoughts and defend her boundaries. She had no intention of allowing him to cast a shadow over her autonomy. The very idea of being spied on—a concept that stirred her indignation—needed to be firmly addressed from their very first meeting.

As she entered the office, the familiar sounds of her workspace surrounded her, but there was an undeniable tension in the air. She scanned the room for any unfamiliar faces, half-hoping they had decided to scrap the whole idea of Jack Archer joining them. The thought of never having to confront him was almost a relief. With a slight furrow in her brow, she made her way to her desk, each step deliberate as she began to gather her files. The scent of freshly brewed coffee wafted through the room, mixed with the subtle smell of paper and ink.

Lucy meticulously organised her caseload, her fingers deftly sorting through the papers and reports. She wanted to project an image of professionalism and competence, ensuring that, should he appear, there would be no doubt in his mind about her capabilities. Strangely, Jack Archer occupied her thoughts like an unwelcome guest—his presence loomed large, igniting a strange blend of intrigue and irritation within her. She couldn't quite unpack why he had such a profound effect on her, but the persistent thought of him ignited a simmering anger that she couldn't shake off. Lucy took a deep breath, summoning her resolve, ready to face whatever the day—and Jack Archer—had in store for her. Almost ready to leave for her first visit of the day, Lucy paused for a moment to bid farewell to her colleagues, exchanging cheerful smiles and friendly waves. At this point, she had assumed that Jack wasn't joining her, and surprisingly, she felt perfectly fine with that.

Suddenly, the door swung open with a gentle creak, and in walked a striking figure: a tall, muscular man with sun-kissed skin that seemed to glow under the overhead lights. His tailored three-piece suit hugged his broad shoulders perfectly, the fabric rich and deep in colour, and he wore a crisp white shirt beneath a meticulously knotted tie. A fitted outer jacket, cut at the three-quarter length, completed his look, highlighting his fit physique.

Lucy's breath caught in her throat for a brief moment as she took in his striking appearance. However, shaking off the surprise, she attempted to walk past him, her gaze focused intently on her bag where she was fumbling for her keys.

Then, his inviting voice broke through the soft clamour of the kitchen, carrying a smooth, slightly posh London accent that seemed to resonate with confidence. "So, which one of you is Lucy then?"

Startled, Lucy looked up, and their eyes met – hers a mix of curiosity and determination, a blend of charm and mischief. The energy shifted in that instant, and she couldn't help but be captivated by the magnetic presence of this enigmatic stranger.

Lucy stormed past Jack, her heels clicking sharply against the floor as she flung the door open with a flourish that radiated defiance. "That would be me, and you're late," she declared, her tone dripping with irritation. With that, she stepped outside, the warm air greeting her as she took a deep breath, trying to cool the fire rising in her chest. Jack trailed behind, his gaze glued to his phone, oblivious to her frustration.

As Lucy scanned the car park, her eyes landed on him, still distracted by the screen. A huff escaped her lips, a mix of annoyance and disbelief. Just then, Jack tucked his phone away, looking up in time to see Lucy unlocking her car. She motioned for him to join her in the passenger seat, her impatience evident.

With a gentle care, Jack opened the door, casting an amused glance over the top of the car. A sunbeam caught his tanned skin, illuminating his perfectly shaven head and making it gleam like polished marble. Those striking blue-grey eyes of his sparkled with mischief, seemingly pulling Lucy in like a magnet and igniting an unexpected shiver down her spine. She quickly shook it off, reminded that she was supposed to be angry with him.

Standing tall, Lucy positioned her hands firmly on her hips, her posture exuding authority and defiance. "You know what," she began, her voice edged with tension, "let's just do this now. I've been told you're here to spy on us, and if that's the case, let me set the record straight: if you have something to say about me, you say it to me. Don't go running to management – they can't solve any issues you think I'm having, can they? Only I can address that. So, before you head off scribbling your reports, you will speak to me first! Got it?!"

Her tone was sharp, every word laced with the heat of her anger, and she maintained an aggressive stance, her gaze locked onto Jack's. But to her surprise, he stood there, a warm and genuine smile spreading across his face, melting her fury away. As she noted the sincerity in his expression, Lucy felt the tension in her body ease, her resolve wavering as she found herself caught in the depths of his mesmerising eyes.

For the rest of the day, the atmosphere between Lucy and Jack shifted dramatically, transforming from tense and uneasy to warm and relaxed. As they moved from one appointment to another, the initial awkwardness melted away, replaced by genuine laughter and engaging conversation. Lucy's eyes sparkled as she shared stories from her childhood, her voice animated with joy, while Jack leaned in, completely captivated, his laughter ringing out like music.

What began as an unlikely pairing had quickly evolved into a delightful friendship. Each visit was sprinkled with humour and shared memories, the two of them weaving their individual tales together until they became an almost seamless narrative of laughter and nostalgia. Their surroundings faded into the background as they revelled in each other's company, even forgetting the workday grind for a while.

The undeniable chemistry between them had sparked like fireworks on New Year's Eve—intense and electrifying—but they both understood the boundaries. Bound by their commitments to others, they made a silent agreement to set those feelings aside and honour their relationships, no matter how strong the pull between them felt.

When they finally stepped back into the office, the atmosphere shifted once more. Colleagues held their breath, a collective pause hanging in the air, expecting to witness the lingering animosity from the morning. Instead, Lucy and Jack walked in side by side, grinning like children who had just shared a delightful secret. Their voices rang out happily, filled with anticipation for another day of collaboration.

Stunned glances were exchanged as everyone processed the sudden change; the transformation was palpable, and even those who tried to look away could see the flickering spark between the two. It danced in the air like a lingering warmth, an unspoken acknowledgment of a connection that was undeniably there, even if they both chose to ignore it for the moment.

Lucy arrived home just as Johnathon was about to step out the door, the late afternoon sun casting a golden hue across the living room. For the first time in a long while, she truly noticed him — the way the soft light caught the warm tones of his hair, how his easy smile seemed to radiate a quiet kindness that filled the room. Johnathon was undeniably a nice man; his heart was as wide as the ocean, though he lacked the eagerness to help that she sometimes yearned for. He wasn't the kind of captivating presence that held her attention the way Jack did, but there was something comforting in his steadiness.

As Johnathon offered her a smile before walking out, Lucy felt a fleeting pang of nostalgia. They had shared countless moments over the years, but recently, their conversations had dwindled to polite exchanges and respectful nods. Time had carved a distance between them, fashioning a friendship that had lost its spark long ago. Instead of nurturing their bond, Lucy had poured herself into her career, chasing ambitions while unwittingly letting their connection slip through her fingers.

Her thoughts wandered frequently to dreams of the extraordinary, especially when she settled down with a cup of coffee and one of her beloved romantic comedies. Lucy often envisioned a dashing knight in shining armour, riding up on a white horse to whisk her away from the ordinary into a world filled with magic and adventure. Though she recognised that those dreams belonged to the realm of fairy tales, the image lingered in her mind like a hopeful whisper.

Suddenly, her thoughts drifted back to Jack. Just the thought of him sent a shiver down her spine. His handsome face filled her mind's eye, the way his dreamy, deep-set eyes seemed to hold secrets untold. His perfect lips — the kind that made time stand still with just a kiss — were forever etched in her memory, alongside his impeccable sense of style that somehow would make every outfit he wore look like a work of art. And oh, the way he smelled! The fragrant mix of Chanel that clung to him like an irresistible spell; it was intoxicating, leaving Lucy breathless.

In that quiet moment, she couldn't deny it any longer: she was smitten. With every heartbeat, she felt the weight of her desires. Lucy realised that deep down, she was still yearning for a spark in her life, a connection that made her heart race and her spirit's soar.

In the coming days, Lucy and Jack found themselves working closely together, their collaboration blossoming into a vibrant synergy. They were drawn to each other, every shared glance igniting a flicker of chemistry that neither could ignore. Yet, both recognised the importance of their burgeoning friendship and made a conscious choice to repress their feelings. They cherished their camaraderie, spending hours exchanging ideas, laughter, and the occasional playful banter.

However, those moments of joy were soon clouded by unease when whispers began to circulate around the office about potential partner switches. A wave of tension swept through Lucy and Jack as they discovered their mutual desire to remain paired together. The thought of separation gnawed at them; Lucy couldn't shake the anxiety of Jack eventually returning to London—a prospect that filled her with dread. It was astonishing to her how deeply she had connected with him after that first, seemingly brutal meeting.

One evening, as Lucy sat enveloped in the soft glow of her living room, the weight of unspoken feelings pressed down on her. She found herself lost in thought, meticulously unravelling the emotions she had begun to associate with Jack. Realising she needed an outlet, she reached for her phone, ready to confide in someone close. Yet, as the ringtone echoed through her house, doubt crept in—was it wise to share such personal revelations about her heart's tumultuous journey?

"Hello?" Dale's familiar voice broke through her haze. "It's been a while; I was starting to wonder if something had happened to you," he chuckled lightly, a sound she had always found comforting.

"Oh... it did!" Lucy replied, her heart pounding in her chest, a mix of excitement and anxiety flooding her senses.

"Okay, not the response I was expecting! Tell me more?" Dale prodded with curiosity.

Taking a deep breath, Lucy let the words flow as she recounted the story of the handsome stranger who had entered her office like a breath of fresh air. She painted a vivid picture of Jack—his charming smile, the way his laughter seemed to light up the room, and how her heart would skip a beat anytime he was near. With every detail she shared, a mixture of exhilaration and apprehension washed over her, challenging her to confront the feelings she had tried so hard to contain.

The advice from Dale had taken Lucy by surprise, steering her thoughts into uncharted territory. She had braced herself for the usual encouragement, perhaps something along the lines of "follow your heart," a platitude she had always found comforting. Instead, Dale offered a grounded perspective that resonated deeply, a voice of reason amid her swirling emotions.

He began by gently reminding her of the years she and Johnathon had spent together, the milestones they had celebrated, and the quiet moments that defined their relationship. As he spoke, Lucy recalled the laughter they shared, the late-night talks that filled their home with warmth, and the intricate tapestry of their shared experiences. Yet, an unsettling truth bubbled up within her: the spark that once ignited their love had dimmed, leaving a lingering sense of emptiness.

Dale pressed on, weaving a narrative about the unpredictable nature of change. He painted a picture of the unknown that lay ahead of her—the thrilling possibility of new beginnings alongside the daunting potential for pain and disappointment. It was a duality that set her heart racing with equal parts of excitement and dread. "You must consider," he stated with sincerity, "the hard work you've put into your career. Navigating a relationship with someone from work could complicate things further, especially if it doesn't pan out. It's a delicate balance, Lucy."

His tone shifted as concern crept into his voice, emphasising that while the choice was ultimately hers to make, he couldn't help but worry. He urged her to approach the idea of pursuing her desires with caution, to dip her toes into the waters rather than plunging in headfirst without considering the currents. It was a pragmatic approach that left a dull ache in her chest.

Though Lucy acknowledged the wisdom in his words, an overwhelming sadness clouded her thoughts. The prospect of abandoning her long-term partner for the promise of something new felt like a betrayal. It gnawed at her; the thought that chasing after a flicker of hope might lead her away from the familiar—away from the security of what she had always known. As days turned into weeks, she grappled with the weight of her dreams, yearning to embrace the possibility of love but tethered to the safety of a relationship that had long ceased to fulfil her.

As Lucy stepped out of her house and into the crisp morning air, a wave of emotions washed over her—a bittersweet pang of sadness intertwined with a sense of clarity. Today marked a turning point; she had made the conscious decision to set aside her lingering dreams of a romance with Jack and focus on nurturing her relationship with Johnathon, a choice that felt both liberating and heavy on her heart.

As she drove, her brother's words echoed in her mind, resonating deeply within her. She sensed that his comments had stemmed from a place of genuine care, a protective instinct fuelled by love for his sister. With that thought, she felt a warm reassurance that perhaps he was right. The heaviness of her past infatuation with Jack gradually began to lift, replaced by the comforting knowledge that she cherished the friendship they had built together.

Lucy relished the connection she and Jack shared; it was a bond that blossomed through laughter-filled conversations and shared interests, a rare gem that she was unwilling to jeopardise by pushing for something more. Every interaction with Jack felt effortless—he brought out her true self, a feeling she treasured deeply. Yet, as much as she enjoyed being with him, she couldn't help but wonder if he saw her in the same light. Jack had never hinted at romantic feelings, and she realised with a tinge of melancholy that he simply enjoyed her company, just as she did his.

With the city bustling around her, Lucy made a quiet determination: she would let go of any romantic fantasies she had harboured and instead embrace the profound friendship they had cultivated. The conversation she had shared with Trisha over the weekend lingered in her thoughts, reinforcing the idea that their connection seemed to be perceived by everyone else as nothing more than a blossoming friendship. It was a perspective that mirrored her brother's insights and gave her pause.

Just because she found herself physically and mentally drawn to Jack didn't guarantee they would make a good couple—such a realisation felt both grounding and freeing. As she approached her workplace, Lucy took a deep breath, ready to shift her focus. She would pour her energy into being the best friend she could be to Jack, cherishing the beautiful camaraderie they shared while releasing the burden of unattainable expectations.

As Lucy stepped into the office that morning, a sense of unease settled over her. The familiar scent of Chanel, which normally wrapped around her like a warm embrace and filled her with anticipation for another day spent alongside Jack, was conspicuously absent. Instead, the sharp, aromatic notes of freshly brewed coffee mingled with the sterile smell of polish, creating an atmosphere that felt foreign and oddly cold.

"Ah, Lucy! Have you heard?" Liam called out, a wide grin stretching across his face. He leaned against the doorframe, his enthusiasm palpable. "They've gone! They've all headed back to London, so we won't be working with them anymore. Apparently, they might come back in a few months, but for now, they've left!" His eyes sparkled with excitement, but Lucy felt a sinking sensation in her stomach.

She couldn't hold back a gasp, her heart racing suddenly. Why hadn't Jack reached out to tell her he was leaving? They had forged a connection amidst the hustle of deadlines and meetings—surely, he owed her at least a heads-up. Though she had always understood that their collaborative work wouldn't last forever, she had hoped for the courtesy of a goodbye, perhaps even a chance to share a drink outside the confines of their office walls, to fortify their bond beyond mere colleagues. But now, he was simply gone, slipping away without a single word.

"Why have they gone?" Lucy asked, her voice barely above a whisper, tinged with confusion and disappointment.

"No idea," Liam replied, his shoulders shrugging nonchalantly. "Apparently, the project they were here for is completed, so it was time for them to return. But you know how it is with us—there are always new recruits coming in, so there's a slim chance they might return at some point. Who knows!" His musings dripped with a casual indifference that grated against her growing sense of loss.

"Oh, okay," Lucy said, her tone laced with resignation. "I thought they would be here longer!" The disappointment hung heavy in the air between them.

Liam chuckled, a teasing glint in his eyes. "Anyone would think you wanted them to stay!"

Lucy disregarded his playful jab, the banter feeling hollow as a lump formed in her throat. She turned on her heel and trudged to her desk, her mind clouded with thoughts as she prepared for the day's work. Though she had resolved to keep her friendship with Jack at a distance, she now feared losing it altogether. The space they had shared within the office felt emptier; the vibrant moments now overshadowed by the sudden silence of his absence.

Lucy spent the next few weeks engulfed in a haze, a strange mixture of nostalgia and longing washing over her like a thick fog. She had Jack's number tucked away in her phone, a constant reminder of the connection they once shared, and the knowledge that he had hers weighed heavily on her mind. But despite this, he hadn't reached out, and each passing day deepened her sense of unease about the prospect of contacting him first. What if he wanted to move on, to leave the remnants of their friendship behind?

She was keenly aware that Jack was back home with his girlfriend, and she couldn't shake the nagging feeling that he might prefer to keep their friendship in the past to avoid unsettling her. Boundaries loomed in her thoughts, a silent wall between them. Yet, the void he left behind felt almost unbearable, both within the office and in the fabric of her daily life. She tried to distract herself, to push the memories of their laughter and profound conversations to the back of her mind, but they crept back, uninvited, invading her every thought.

As Lucy sat alone in her dimly lit living room, the silence seemed to amplify her internal conflict. She wrapped her arms around her knees, grateful for the warmth of the blanket draped over her legs, but it offered little comfort against the chill of uncertainty. Contemplation danced through her mind like a trapped firefly—should she reach out to Jack? What words could encapsulate her feelings? Would he even reply? Or had their time together truly faded into a mere memory?

Eventually, Lucy settled on the uncomfortable notion that the only way to quell her uncertainties was to take a leap of faith. With a deep breath, she pulled out her phone, the screen illuminating her face in the dim room. She hesitated for a moment, fingers hovering over the keys as she searched for the right words to bridge the gap that had grown between them. "Hi Jack, I really hope you are well," she began, her heart pounding. "I was really disappointed when they told me you had gone back to London, as I genuinely enjoyed working together." She kept typing, pouring her sentiments into the message, determined to express her gratitude. "Anyway, I wanted to take this opportunity to say thank you for being such a good partner over the last few months, and I would love to work with you again in the future should the opportunity ever arise."

As she crafted her message, the anxious voice in her head kept telling her that she might sound desperate or that she should say something more casual. After what felt like an endless cycle of writing and deleting, Lucy finally crafted a message that felt true to her. With a deep, wavering breath, she hit send and set her phone down beside her, heart racing as the silence in the room enveloped her once more. Would he reply? Would he want to keep in touch? The questions lingered in her mind, filling the quiet as she anxiously awaited a response.

After nearly two weeks had slipped by, a heavy sense of resignation settled over Lucy as she convinced herself that Jack must no longer wish to keep in touch. The silence from him was deafening; no texts, no calls, nothing at all. It perplexed her, considering the strong bond they had forged while working side by side, sharing laughter and late-night projects. Those memories had felt warm and vibrant, but now they seemed to fade like distant echoes, leaving her with a gnawing doubt that perhaps their friendship held little significance for him.

Determined to push away the unsettling thoughts, Lucy buried herself in her work. The clatter of keyboard strokes became a temporary refuge, drowning out the whispers of longing and disappointment that cluttered her mind. She forced Jack to the farthest corners of her thoughts, convincing herself that if he truly wanted to cut ties, it must mean their connection was insubstantial. Resolute, she decided to focus on her career, banishing any notions of what might have been—a friendship or even something deeper.

Her relationship with Johnathon lingered on the periphery, dull but steady, threatening to reach its inevitable conclusion. Yet, Lucy found herself clinging to the familiar, even if she was growing weary of it. At least with Johnathon, she enjoyed a semblance of reliability; he would respond promptly to her messages, unlike Jack, who had vanished without a trace. But in the quiet corners of her mind, Lucy recognised the flawed reasoning behind her feelings—she wasn't in a romantic relationship with Jack, merely a colleague with whom she had shared moments of camaraderie.

As she reflected on her situation, the realisation crept in her perspective was warped. Jack was just a work companion with whom she had exchanged laughs, and the fantasies of friendship or romance were illusions she had crafted to fill the void.

Chapter Five

It had now been weeks since Lucy's failed attempt to contact Jack, a memory that lingered like a shadow in the corners of her mind. She had managed to shove him to the back of her thoughts, almost managing to forget about him altogether—but not quite. Instead, she found herself increasingly drawn to Liam, a man who had woven himself into the fabric of her daily life. Their friendship blossomed through shared cups of coffee and laughter echoing in the office break room, where the air was often filled with the rich aroma of freshly brewed espresso and the chatter of colleagues.

Liam, with his strikingly dark polished features and impeccable sense of style, was the kind of man who turned heads. His crisp dress shirts and tailored suits accentuated his confident demeanour, making him a magnet for attention among the ladies. Yet, despite his charm and undeniable good looks, Lucy felt no spark of attraction towards him. While they shared moments of genuine laughter, she often found herself stifling yawns at his steadfastness and unwavering adherence to the rules.

Lucy had always relished the thrill of bending the rules, a rebellious spirit that had been evident even in her childhood. The mere thought of breaking free from the confines of conformity sent a rush of adrenaline coursing through her veins, and she would often have to summon all her willpower to stifle her impulses when circumstances demanded restraint. Liam, on the other hand, was like a well-worn path, predictable and safe, and that predictability, in many ways, dulled her excitement.

In the evenings, when the sun dipped below the horizon, painting the sky in banners of pink and orange, Liam would often call Lucy just to check in. Their conversations were light-hearted and filled with warmth, a balm against the solitude of her evenings. Although Lucy was acutely aware that Liam held a romantic interest in her, she remained resolute in her stance. The idea of pursuing anything beyond friendship with him felt as unappealing as trying to fit a square peg into a round hole. She cherished their companionship but desired nothing more than that—solid, uncomplicated, and free of the tangled web of romantic entanglements. As the sun began its descent, casting a warm glow over the office, Liam approached Lucy with an air of playful anticipation. "Hey, do you want to grab a coffee with me?" he asked, a hint of excitement in his voice. Lucy paused, reflecting on the monotony of her daily routine—heading home to engage in trivial conversations with Johnathon that barely scratched the surface of her thoughts—and, feeling a spark of spontaneity, she readily agreed.

They strolled through the lively streets, the aromas of coffee wafting from the shop just a couple of hundred yards away. Upon entering the cosy café, they found a small table near the window, where they could watch the world bustle by. As Liam headed to the counter, Lucy took off her coat, revealing a simple but elegant outfit that spoke to her understated style. Noticing the remnants of previous customers scattered across the table, she took it upon herself to clear away the clutter, making the space inviting for their conversation.

When Liam returned, a confident grin danced on his lips as he placed a beautifully crafted vanilla latte in front of her. "There you go, vanilla latte just the way you like it!" he said, his eyes twinkling with genuine warmth. Lucy's heart fluttered as she accepted the cup, grateful he remembered her fondness for the sweet, creamy drink. "Thanks! I didn't think you'd recall. It's been ages since we shared a coffee like this," she replied, her voice tinged with a hint of nostalgia.

As they settled into the rhythm of their conversation, Lucy started to feel the unmistakable current of flirtation that Liam expertly wove into his words. His compliments were light yet layered with meaning, each one making Lucy both blush and squirm inwardly. She chose to sidestep his advances for the moment; she valued their friendship too much to risk complicating it with misplaced intentions, though his charm certainly set her heart racing.

After finishing their drinks, the air was thick with the unspoken tension that lingered between them. Liam leaned closer, his eyes glimmering with a mix of mischief and curiosity as he invited her back to his plush apartment. Lucy felt a rush of unease at the suggestion. She cherished the bond they shared but sensed that he might have something else in mind, something she wasn't prepared to entertain. With a gentle yet firm smile, she declined, feeling a rush of relief mixed with disappointment at the crossing of boundaries that she wasn't ready to navigate. "I need to get home now; Johnathon will be waiting for me!" Lucy exclaimed, her tone a mix of urgency and polite deflection as she sidestepped Liam's offer. She could feel the heat rising in her cheeks, a telltale sign of her embarrassment. "That's a shame!" Liam replied, his voice laced with a hint of mischief that made her pulse quicken. He shot her a playful wink, his smile hinting at the fun he had imagined they could share. As he stood up and slid his fitted jacket back on, Lucy felt a swell of relief wash over her — he hadn't pushed the matter further, sparing her from any further awkwardness.

They walked towards the door together, a shared silence hanging between them, until Lucy decided to break away. "I just have to go and get something, so I will see you later" she said, forcing a casual tone as she veered off in another direction, her heart racing from the near miss.

Once home, a sense of relief enveloped Lucy like a warm blanket. She had managed to navigate the potentially awkward situation with Liam without any major fallout, and it served as a lesson for her moving forward. She realised that declining coffee invites after work might be wise for now. For some time, she had sensed Liam's interest in her, but she hadn't anticipated that he might believe there was a chance for something more between them.

The house was blissfully quiet, with Johnathon already gone until the following morning; he had mentioned earlier that day his plans to visit a friend's house tonight. Lucy cherished these moments of solitude, a rare chance to unwind and indulge in her favourite activities. She had envisioned a delightful evening filled with a long, luxurious bubble bath, fragrant face masks, a deep conditioning hair treatment, a feel-good movie, and a soothing glass of wine to truly escape into relaxation.

Just as Lucy settled into her thoughts, her phone chimed, breaking the silence. She picked it up to find a message from Jack. The screen lit up with his name as she read the heartfelt note: "Hi Lucy, I had to leave in a hurry as I received some terrible news — a friend of mine passed away, and I needed to head back to London to help his wife with the funeral arrangements, and of course, to attend the funeral. I genuinely enjoyed our time working together, and I would love the chance to collaborate again in the future. When I return to the office, I'll ask to be paired with you again. I'm not sure when that will be, though, as I have a lot on my plate right now. I have another job as well, which keeps me quite busy and is why my replies take me some time. Anyway, I hope to hear from you again soon."

As Lucy read his message, she felt a mix of emotions — sympathy for Jack amidst his sorrow, a tingle of excitement at the thought of working with him again, and the familiar warmth of connection they had shared before. Lucy sat in her small but cosy living room, the soft glow of the lamp casting a warm light across the room. She reread Jack's message; her heart heavy with empathy. Each word felt like a whisper, carrying the weight of his loss. Finally, she began to compose her reply, pouring her heart into the message: "Aww, I'm so sorry for your loss, Jack. I had no idea. I did wonder why you disappeared all of a sudden, but I figured it was just work, not something as terrible as that. I hope you are okay, and please pass on my condolences to his family too. I know I didn't know him, but it's always sad to hear someone has passed away, isn't it? I will definitely look forward to you coming back to us!"

As she pressed send, a rush of relief washed over her. The thought of Jack reaching out had ignited a sense of joy within her, a beacon of connection amid the sombre news. She couldn't shake the fear of losing that connection, of drifting away from someone she had so admired. Sitting on the edge of her seat, she glanced anxiously at her phone, the silence in the room amplifying her anticipation. Minutes dripped by slowly, stretching into an hour, and her heart sank as Jack didn't reply.

The bubble bath she had planned, filled with fragrant lavender and soft candlelight, seemed less inviting now. Instead, she decided to distract herself by calling Trisha. As the phone rang, Lucy felt a blend of excitement and apprehension, eager to share her thoughts on both her own burgeoning feelings for Jack and the ongoing drama with Liam.

"Hey, Lucy! You sound different," Trisha's voice chirped through the receiver, but that sparkle of enthusiasm quickly dimmed as Lucy unravelled her news. "I know you think you know what you're doing but just make sure you've really thought this through!"

Lucy frowned, her brows furrowing in confusion. "Thought what through? We are only talking; we're friends, just like you and me. It's nothing more. I just enjoy talking to him, that's all!"

Trisha's silence spoke volumes, and Lucy could practically hear her rolling her eyes. She knew her friend was worried, sensing the undercurrents that Lucy seemed blissfully unaware of. But Lucy's resolve was firm; she cherished her conversations with Jack and was unwilling to relinquish that joy.

"Lucy, you're a big girl and will make whatever decision you make, but just tread carefully, is all I'm saying!" Trisha's tone was laced with concern, but it only strengthened Lucy's desire to forge her own path.

"Thanks, Trisha," Lucy replied, a soft smile creeping onto her face despite the tension in the air. "I miss you too!" she added, knowing that their friendship would always be a safe haven. Then, as the call ended, she placed her phone down and glanced out the window at the softly falling dusk, her thoughts still tangled in the complexities of connection, friendship, and the fragile lines that could so easily blur in the quiet of her heart.

For the next two weeks, every time Lucy's phone chimed, a pang of anticipation surged through her, a flicker of hope sparking within her chest at the thought that it might be Jack reaching out. Yet, disappointment followed each time as she unlocked her screen to find only unremarkable notifications. With her brow furrowed in thought, she reminisced about his earlier text, where he mentioned juggling another job that consumed much of his time. What could this mystery job be? The ambiguity gnawed at her curiosity; he had shared so little, merely alluding to the demands it placed on his schedule. Lucy speculated that perhaps this was the reason for his radio silence, a conclusion that swirled around in her mind like leaves caught in a gust of wind.

Just when Lucy decided to release the hope of receiving a message, her phone lit up with a notification from Jack. She was with a client at the time, and her heart raced as she caught sight of his name flashing across the screen. All she yearned for was to delve into his words, but her professional decorum prevented her from doing so while the appointment lingered on. A knot of impatience tightened in her stomach, and she found herself hurrying through the remaining minutes with her client, the rhythm of her thoughts loud and chaotic, consumed by what Jack might have to say.

The moment the appointment ended, Lucy was quick to slip her phone from her pocket, barely registering her surroundings as she walked toward the car, her eyes glued to the screen. Jack's message unfolded before her eyes, rich with tales of his daily grind, peppered with anecdotes that made her chuckle amid the weight of the words. But a shadow loomed in the text as he recounted the sombre story of the funeral he had recently attended for a close friend. It was a long, heartfelt message, one that clearly reflected the time and care he had poured into it.

Lucy's fingers itched to respond immediately, but just as she prepared to type, the shrill ring of the office phone jolted her back to reality. She had to prioritise her responsibilities, updating her boss on the appointments she'd completed and the schedule ahead. Frustration tinged her voice, rising like a tide as she navigated the conversation, but a determined resolve nestled deep within her. All she craved was to end the call and dive into her thoughts, to craft a reply to Jack before the delicate moment faded before the silence between them grew even heavier.

Once the call had finished, Lucy took a deep breath and began to carefully craft her message. She poured her heart into each word, recounting the trials and tribulations of the clients they had once visited together, her mind flashing back to the long meetings and late-night brainstorming sessions that had forged their bond. With a vivid imagination, she painted stories of her recent escapades outside of work, weaving in snippets about her friend Trisha, her carefree laughter, and the mischief they often got into, as well as tales of her brother Dale, whose uncanny ability to always land in peculiar situations never failed to amuse her.

As Lucy typed her response, she aimed to mirror the depth and richness of Jack's previous message, hoping to evoke the same warmth and camaraderie that had grown between them. When she reached the end of her message, she initially signed off with a playful 'x,' but a moment's hesitation crept in. Nervously, she deleted it, afraid that such familiarity might lead him to misconstrue her intentions and pull away from their friendship. She had always made a point to ask about his girlfriend, genuinely concerned for her well-being, but if she were honest, she was seeking to gauge the health of their relationship. Jack would typically respond with a brief reassurance that she was fine, providing little else, and though it was enough for Lucy, it left a subtle ache within her—a haunting reminder that this woman had what she secretly desired.

Days turned into weeks, and the silence from Jack began to linger like an uninvited guest in her life. Each day, Lucy found herself checking her phone, hoping for a message that never came, her mind spinning with the possibility that she had said something wrong, mis stepped in their delicate friendship. The year and a half they had spent forging their connection now felt fragile and distant, strained by the lack of communication.

Finally, in an effort to shake off the unease and regain a sense of control, Lucy resolved to take a break from it all. She opened her laptop, the bright screen illuminated her face, casting a gentle glow in the dimly lit room. She began to search for flights to sunny Spain, her heart racing at the thought of escaping the cocoon of uncertainty. The time had come for her to unwind, to soak up the sun, and to immerse herself in laughter and adventures with her best friend, far away from the whispers of doubt that had settled uncomfortably in her mind.

Chapter Six

As the plane gently touched down on the sun-soaked Spanish runway, a thrill of excitement coursed through Lucy's veins, igniting a spark of energy that had been dormant during the long flight. The moment the wheels hit the tarmac, she could feel the anticipation bubbling up inside her, like a joyous wave ready to crash. It had been far too long since she and Trisha had shared any real time together, and now the sweet reunion was finally within reach.

Only a few days prior, Trisha had called with elation, her voice practically dancing through the phone as Lucy announced her visit. The two had been nearly inseparable during their years working together and this trip promised to rekindle that vibrant friendship. Trisha had assured Lucy that she would be at the airport to greet her personally, refusing to let her best friend navigate the unfamiliar terrain of Spanish taxis alone. Trisha's eagerness was palpable, she couldn't wait to show off her shiny, new car—an extravagant gift from her fiancé, affectionately dubbed 'Mr. Perfect.'

Mr. Perfect was not just a romantic figure; he was also the successful proprietor of bustling hotels in Spain. The establishments had flourished under his stewardship, generating enough wealth to allow Trisha to live a life of leisure. Lucy couldn't help but feel a twinge of jealousy—who wouldn't want to be swept away by such fortune? Yet, alongside that pang of envy was an overwhelming sense of happiness for her friend. Trisha deserved every bit of this, and Lucy was thrilled to see her basking in the fruits of her success.

Unbelievably, Trisha had made the decision to retire early—a concept that once seemed like a fantasy, hovering just out of reach.

Now, in her fifties, she was luxuriating in her newfound freedom, unburdened by the responsibilities of teaching. The reality of it all filled Lucy with a sense of wonder; they would finally be able to spend quality time together without the constraints of busy schedules.

As she stepped off the plane, Lucy was greeted by the brilliant Spanish sun, which enveloped her in its warmth like a long-lost friend. The sky above was painted in a vivid blue, unmarred by clouds, and a gentle warm breeze danced across her face, carrying with it the sweet scent of blooming flowers. She paused for a moment, soaking it all in, before quickening her pace to catch up with the throngs of other passengers. Their purposefulness seemed reassuring, a reminder that she was no longer a stranger here; she was stepping into the next chapter of her best friend's adventure.

"Oh my god, you're finally here!" Trisha screamed, her voice bubbling with excitement as she dashed toward Lucy, her arms outstretched. The moment their bodies met in an embrace; it felt as if the world around them faded away. Lucy returned the hug with equal enthusiasm, squeezing Trisha tightly as if to make up for all the time they had missed. "I know, can you believe it?" Lucy replied, her eyes sparkling with exhilaration. "I couldn't wait any longer; I needed to get my ass over here and check out your empire once and for all!"

Trisha's face lit up, radiating joy. "Oh, you are going to love it, I promise!" she declared, her voice full of warmth. The excitement swirling in the air was palpable, but underneath it lay anticipation for a more significant moment—Lucy was about to meet 'Mr. Perfect,' the man Trisha had often gushed about—Pablo. Trisha could hardly contain her eagerness to introduce them, but for now, she had to wait. Pablo was ensnared in a crucial business meeting, discussing the purchase of a third hotel, a sign of his burgeoning success.

As Trisha explained this to Lucy, the shock registered on Lucy's face. "I'm sorry, what? A third hotel?" she exclaimed, her voice a blend of disbelief and awe. Trisha nodded, an impressed smile gracing her lips as she marvelled at her fiancé's accomplishments. "Yeah, I know! He bought the second one just last year!" she elaborated, her pride evident in her tone.

"How come you didn't tell me?" asked Lucy, feeling the weight of her friend's achievements press down on her.

Trisha rolled her eyes playfully. "Well, Lucy, lately every conversation we've had seems to revolve around the one and only, very same subject of the elusive colleague Jack, hasn't it?" she replied, a hint of exasperation mixed with affection in her voice.

In that moment, a wave of guilt washed over Lucy. Her mind raced as she reflected on their recent chats, suddenly aware of how consumed she had been by her own troubles. Trisha, who had so much happening in her own life, deserved more attention than Lucy had given. As realisation set in, Lucy felt a pang in her chest. She was overwhelmed with a sense of regret for not being there for her best friend during this exciting chapter. In that shared hug filled with joy, she now bore the burden of feeling like a terrible friend.

As they cruised through the sun-soaked streets of Spain, Lucy felt a surge of excitement as she absorbed the vibrant landscape around her. The terracotta buildings, with their sun-bleached stucco and wrought iron balconies adorned with colourful flower boxes, seemed to paint a picturesque backdrop against the clear blue sky. Towering palm trees swayed gently in the warm breeze, casting playful shadows on the cobbled pavements. Each turn of the road revealed charming cafes, with the enticing aroma of rich coffee and freshly baked pastries wafting through the air, making Lucy's mouth water.

She couldn't help but marvel at how Trisha got to experience this enchanting place every day; it felt surreal to be there herself. Lucy had booked this two-week escape, yearning for a break to switch off from the relentless demands of her work and the weighty presence of Johnathon, who had been anything but supportive about her decision to travel solo.

When she had mentioned her trip, Johnathon's reaction had been predictable. He had launched into a lecture about responsibilities and the importance of shared holidays, as if every minute spent apart, was a betrayal. Lucy sighed at the memory; their past vacations had turned into a frustrating ritual. Johnathon would insist on meandering into town, perusing shops filled with trinkets and baubles that caught his eye but served no real purpose. He would purchase these pointless items with the fervour of a collector, leaving Lucy to fester in a growing irritation. The rest of the time, he would retreat to their hotel room, air conditioning blasting, glued to the television while Lucy felt trapped in a cycle of compromise.

In that moment, Lucy was blissfully removed from those worries, seated in Trisha's sleek, bright red convertible with the roof down. The wind whipped through her hair, a delightful mess of freedom and fluttering strands, and Trisha had thoughtfully given her a chic headscarf before their departure. It fluttered around her head like a soft embrace, providing a touch of elegance against the exhilaration of the open road. With every mile they drove, the weight of her everyday life began to lift, replaced by the promise of adventure and relaxation that lay ahead.

As Trisha navigated her car along the winding, tree-lined driveway, secured by sleek electronic gates that whispered shut behind them, Lucy felt a sense of awe wash over her. Before her stood an impressive two-story detached house, a grand testament to Trisha's success, surrounded by sprawling acres of meticulously tended land. The gardens bloomed in a riot of colours, vibrant flowers peeking through lush greenery, their petals kissed by the sun, creating a living canvas that danced with life. Lucy was utterly entranced by Trisha's home; the pictures she had seen were merely glimpses of the paradise that unfolded before her.

Entering the house, Lucy was greeted by the cool elegance of pristine white marble floors that gleamed under the gentle glow of recessed lighting. The lofty ceilings soared above them, accentuated by exquisite crown moulding that framed the walls like a work of art. The décor was a harmonious blend of modern sophistication and comfort, each room meticulously curated with the finest furniture that spoke of both style and luxury. "Wow!" Lucy exclaimed; her voice filled with wonder as her eyes roamed over the carefully chosen decor. "It's absolutely beautiful!"

Standing beside her, Trisha exuded confidence, her perfectly tanned skin glowing like warm honey. She looked almost Mediterranean, especially with her stylish headscarf and the flowing floral dress that embraced her curves, embodying both grace and femininity.

"I can't believe this is your home; it's like a dream!" Lucy breathed, her heart swelling with admiration.

"Right...!" Trisha replied with a playful grin, her eyes sparkling with excitement. "Let's crack open the wine, shall we?"

They made their way into the expansive kitchen, a blend of contemporary design with rustic charm. The sleek lines of the cabinetry contrasted with an inviting old-country-style wooden seating area, where worn patina told tales of family gatherings and laughter. It was a touch of nostalgia that reflected Trisha's countryside roots, a reminder of where she had come from and the warmth that still lingered in her heart.

Lucy and Trisha spent the rest of the evening savouring the rich wine, its velvety texture swirling in their glasses as they reminisced about the past two years of separation. With each sip, Lucy felt the weight of her troubles with Johnathon and the cool distance she had with Jack fade into the background, replaced by the warmth and tranquillity that enveloped Trisha's stunning home. The soft glow of the sun setting flickered against the walls, casting gentle shadows as laughter and heartfelt stories filled the air, creating a comforting atmosphere that wrapped around them like a cherished blanket.

The following days were a delightful adventure as the two friends explored the enchanting surroundings. They wandered through charming cobblestone streets that wound between quaint local shops, indulging in artisanal pastries at the little coffee nooks adorned with colourful tiles. Each wine bar they visited revealed its unique character, filled with the laughter of patrons and the enticing aromas of local delicacies, enriching their experience with the vibrant culture that surrounded them.

Amidst all the exploration, a shadow of curiosity lingered in Lucy's mind—she hadn't yet crossed paths with Pablo. Initially, she had anticipated meeting him on her first night in Spain, but fate had other plans. Pablo seemed to be a mirage, returning home long after she had settled into her room for the night and leaving for work at dawn while she still lingered in the realm of sleep. Each missed encounter piqued her curiosity, and she couldn't help but wonder how much of Pablo her best friend truly got to enjoy, given his constant preoccupation with the hotels. Yet, she hesitated to voice her thoughts, not wanting to disrupt the harmony of the moment.

Finally, on the fourth night of her trip, the moment she had awaited arrived. Lucy and Trisha ventured to The Grand Siesta, Pablo's first hotel, a magnificent five-story terracotta structure that stood proudly against the backdrop of the dusky sky. Its elegant façade hinted at the charm hidden within, each room graced with its own balcony that overlooked the bustling streets below. The décor was understated yet inviting, embodying a clean simplicity that made the space feel welcoming.

They made their way to the bar area, which was quaint and intimate, with only four bar stools perfectly positioned along the polished wooden countertop. As they settled onto their stools, Lucy felt the anticipation in the air. Trisha, with a playful glint in her eye, conversed in rapid Spanish with the bartender, her words flowing like music, but Lucy only caught fragments amidst the melodic sounds. Then came the wink—a knowing signal that something was about to unfold.

In an instant, two vibrant strawberry daiquiris appeared before them, their bright pink hues glistening in the neon lighting. The refreshing scent of fresh fruit floated in the air, mingling with hints of rum and lime. With laughter bubbling between them, they raised their glasses in a toast, clinking them together in celebration of friendship and new beginnings, before savouring the sweet and tangy concoctions, each sip amplifying the shared joy of their long-awaited reunion. They must have sat there sipping their vibrant cocktails, each drink bursting with colours and flavours, for a good couple of hours. The atmosphere around them was alive with laughter and clinking glasses, a true testament to the joy of the moment. Just as the sun dipped below the horizon, casting a warm golden glow over everything, a tall stranger emerged from the throng. His skin glistened like polished mahogany, and his perfectly trimmed beard framed a chiselled face adorned with thick, black curls cropped closely to his head. With an effortless charm, he approached Trisha, his presence commanding attention.

He planted a hand on her hip, an intimate gesture, before leaning down to plant a tender kiss on the top of her head. "My darling man!" cried Trisha, her eyes sparkling with excitement as she turned to face him, the connection between them palpable. She responded to him with another kiss—this time on his perfectly formed lips, a brief moment that seemed to encapsulate the affection they shared.

Pablo then turned to Lucy, a warm smile spreading across his face as he extended his hand in greeting. Lucy felt a flutter of nerves as she raised her hand to shake his, but Pablo graciously lifted her hand to his mouth and planted a gentle kiss on the back of it. "And this must be the beautiful Lucy!" he exclaimed, his voice rich and melodic, laced with charisma.

A blush crept up Lucy's cheeks, an involuntary response to the unexpected compliment, and she couldn't help but feel slightly embarrassed under the weight of his gaze. "You are even more beautiful than Trisha described you!" he continued, his smile illuminating the space around him. His words were like soft petals falling in a gentle breeze, comforting and sweet.

He then turned back to Trisha, his eyes sparkling with love as he stared deeply into hers. "But nobody will ever be as beautiful as my fiancé, I'm afraid," he said, a hint of playfulness in his tone. The sentiment washed over Lucy, alleviating the unease that had settled in her stomach. She had wondered what their relationship was like, and now, witnessing the affection between them, she had her answer. It was a beautiful thing, filled with warmth and genuine love, giving Lucy a sense of ease she hadn't realised she needed.

Following the meeting with Pablo, the remainder of Lucy's trip seemed to drift by like a soft summer breeze. As she nestled into the inviting embrace of a swing, surrounded by the vibrant blooms of Trisha's beautifully manicured garden, she savoured the sweet tang of her cocktail. The warm evening sun painted everything into a golden mist, and the gentle rustle of leaves created a serene backdrop for her thoughts. However, amidst the tranquillity, a nagging worry crept into her mind— it had been a good few weeks since she had last heard from Jack.

Had he decided to cut ties entirely, perhaps feeling that their connection wasn't worth pursuing? Had she unintentionally said something to push him away? The uncertainty gnawed at her. Deep down, Lucy realised that if Jack truly wished to distance himself, there was little she could do to change his mind.

In contrast, her daily interactions with Johnathon while she was away had been nothing more than casual check-ins – light conversations that lacked the spark to brighten her days. As she soaked in the perfect silence of the garden, each moment felt bittersweet.

Just then, her phone chimed, breaking the spell of her reverie. With a flutter of anticipation, Lucy glanced at the screen—it was a message from Jack. A surprising rush of adrenaline coursed through her, as she suddenly realised, she had forgotten the content of her last message to him. In that moment, it didn't matter; the possibility of reconnecting filled her with a mixture of hope and trepidation, stirring emotions that she thought she had set aside. The evening seemed to hold its breath, waiting for her next move. "Hey! I'm really sorry it's taken me so long to get back to you. I had to leave for work with my other job, and unfortunately, I ended up being away for the past four weeks. It's been quite a whirlwind. While I was gone, I had a pretty serious incident where some metal ended up lodged in my arm. It was a pretty scary situation, having to get it removed, and now that it's healing, I'm left with a rather unusual scar that tells a story of its own. On top of that, I managed to fracture my ulna when the shrapnel hit, so I'm currently stuck in a cast.

It's safe to say things became quite hectic, and I wanted to wait until life calmed down a bit before reaching out. Now that I'm back home and settled back in the office, I thought it was time to drop you a quick message to let you know I'm okay. How have you been? What's been going on in your life?"

As Lucy contemplated his message, she felt a twinge of resentment. Did he really have a right to enquire about her life after being absent for so long? But then, guilt washed over her as she thought about the ordeal he must have endured. It left her curious about the mysterious job that had pulled him away for weeks. What could possibly require someone to face such dangers? Lucy made a deliberate choice not to respond with a straightforward text message. Instead, she opted to send a breathtaking photograph she had taken from the upstairs window of the hotel during their visit. The image captured a lively nightlife scene, with twinkling lights reflecting off the surface of the water. The beach below was bathed in the warm, golden hues of dusk, where the waves gently lapped at the shore, leaving shimmering trails in their wake.

She figured she wouldn't hear back from Jack anytime soon, so she decided to wait until she was sober and had a clearer sense of what her reply should be. Just as she was lost in these thoughts, her phone chimed again, startling her. To her surprise, it was another message from Jack. "Wow that looks lovely, where are you?" he enquired, his words filled with genuine curiosity.

Seizing the moment, Lucy decided it was time to respond. She poured her feelings into her message, hoping it would spark a meaningful conversation. "It truly is lovely here! The weather has been absolutely stunning; the sun shines brightly, and the gentle breeze carries the scent of the sea. I'm currently in Spain, soaking up the sun and spending time with my best friend, the one I mentioned to you. Unfortunately, I'll be flying home in three days. Honestly, I feel like I could just stay here forever; it's so breathtakingly beautiful!" her message read, filled with warmth and longing for the vibrant atmosphere surrounding her.

Lucy didn't receive another message from Jack after her last thoughtful reply. As she boarded the plane headed home, an unexpected wave of melancholy washed over her; leaving her friend felt like leaving a piece of her heart behind. Yet, amidst that sadness, there was a flicker of joy for Trisha—her friend's life seemed to be unfolding in vibrant colours, filled with the promise of love and happiness alongside Pablo.

Lucy adored flying—the sensation of lift-off, the hum of the engines, and the mesmerising view of the world shrinking beneath her always filled her with a sense of adventure. Settling into her seat, she felt her heart race with excitement and anticipation for the journey ahead. The plane taxied, and as it hurtled down the runway, a rush of adrenaline surged through her. Suddenly, they were airborne, and the cloud-dappled sky enveloped her, making her troubles feel a little lighter.

Before she realised it, the flight had flown by, seemingly in the blink of an eye. The wheels touched down with a gentle thud, and as she gathered her luggage, a mix of eagerness and apprehension swirled within her while she awaited Johnathon's arrival to pick her up.

Once in Johnathon's car, the familiar scents of leather and an air freshener filled her senses. Lucy began recounting her tales of Trisha and Pablo—how they had laughed, danced, and celebrated their friendship under the sun-drenched skies. As she painted vivid pictures with her words, her heart sank as she reflected on her own relationship. The lingering warmth of their happiness highlighted the chill of her own solitude. She had sensed for some time that the affection between her and Johnathon had been waning, but being reminded of Trisha and Pablo's electric connection made the stark contrast undeniable.

With each anecdote, Lucy's realisation deepened; she had to confront the growing void in her own life. A pang of determination surged within her—she knew she needed to act and seek change. Now, the only question was how and when she would muster the courage to make it happen.

Back at work, the atmosphere buzzed with warmth and camaraderie, but Lucy's presence added a captivating glow to the environment. Her beautifully tanned skin seemed to draw everyone's gaze, particularly from Liam, whose admiration was evident in his bright, hopeful eyes. He would hover near her, never missing an opportunity to extol her beauty, his voice tinged with genuine awe as he remarked on her radiant complexion and enviable figure. Each compliment felt like a small intimacy, yet Lucy found herself caught in a web of polite refusals as Liam repeatedly suggested that they go out for drinks together.

Inside, Lucy wrestled with her emotions. At home, affection was scarce, and discontent had taken root in her heart, leaving a longing that was hard to ignore. The allure of Liam's attention was undeniably tempting, yet she knew succumbing to it would complicate her already unsettled life. Meanwhile, her interactions with Jack were far less frequent, limited to the odd message exchanged every couple of weeks. His stories, filled with adventure and a sense of danger, painted a vivid picture of his travels abroad. Jack would regale her with tales about working with offenders in exotic locales, his diverse language skills allowing him to navigate a world stirred with uncertainty.

Yet, beneath the adventurous facade, Lucy felt a twinge of anxiety. His stories sometimes seemed too outrageous to be true and often left her wrapped in worry. What if one day, he ventured too far and didn't return? Or worse, came back altered by experiences too dark to share? The thoughts were stark, yet they mixed with her enjoyment of his messages, a bittersweet reminder of her place in his life. Lucy came to realise that her connection with Jack would likely never evolve past friendship, an understanding that cast a shadow over her thoughts. Despite the warmth of his words, something told her the distance between them was insurmountable.

Chapter Seven

Lucy's mind began to whirl like a turbulent storm as she read Jack's latest message. The conversation had picked up over the weekend, a flurry of texts that ignited a mix of emotions within her. Jack had shared the news that he and his girlfriend had ended their relationship six months prior, a revelation that sent a flicker of hope through Lucy's heart. But that brief spark quickly extinguished as he mentioned meeting someone new—a woman he connected with instantly while working.

A pang of jealousy coursed through her veins, sharp and bitter. She had harboured a secret wish that Jack's breakup would finally open a door for her, a chance to step into a potentially deeper connection. Yet, with each message, her hopes felt like sand slipping through her fingers. He was moving on, and she felt stuck in her feelings, grounded by the weight of unspoken emotions. The mention of his new love interest tugged at her heartstrings, leaving her with a bittersweet taste of sorrow.

Despite the tumult within, Lucy chose to mask her disappointment with a smile. She sent her congratulations, filled with encouragement for his new pursuit, wanting nothing more than to see him happy—even if it wasn't with her. It struck her how long it had been since they had last seen each other, nearly a year and a half. Their relationship had transitioned from the warmth of friendship to a series of digital exchanges, more like pen pals lost in the vastness of the online world.

As Jack's words echoed in her mind, Lucy began to ponder her own feelings, a slow realisation blooming within her. Perhaps now was the moment to speak to Johnathon about what had been lingering in her heart for far too long. She felt the stirrings of possibility; maybe this was her chance to explore her own feelings, to step into the unknown with courage, just as Jack had. Lucy sat on the edge of the couch, the soft fabric enveloping her but offering little comfort. The dim light of the living room cast long shadows against the walls as she replayed the afternoon's conversation with Dale in her mind. It had been two hours filled with soul-bearing honesty, where she laid bare her feelings of discontent and frustration. Dale, with his calm demeanour, had listened intently, his support reassuring her as he encouraged her to pursue her own happiness.

Tonight, she decided, was the night she would confront Johnathon. The thought sent a shiver down her spine, a mix of fear and determination swirling within her. She had felt a tight knot in her stomach all day, knowing that she was about to shatter the fragile facade of their life together. The security that their relationship offered was a double-edged sword, providing comfort while simultaneously suffocating her spirit. She couldn't shake the thought that, despite the fear of losing that stability, it was vital she spoke her truth.

As Lucy anxiously awaited Johnathon's return, an unsettling doubt crept in, fluttering through her mind like a dark butterfly. What if tonight wasn't the right time? What if she waited for another day, a moment when her courage wasn't so intertwined with dread?

Just then, she heard the familiar sound of tyres crunching over gravel as Johnathon's car pulled up outside. Her heart raced as he killed the engine, the stillness after the roar of the motor amplifying her anxiety. He stepped out of the car, locking it with a mechanical click that echoed in her ears. When he entered the house, he wore the weight of the world on his shoulders, his brow furrowed as he muttered, "Alright?" in a tone steeped in irritation.

"Yeah, are you?" Lucy replied, trying to keep her voice steady, though it felt shaky.

Johnathon let loose a tirade of complaints about work, traffic, and the mundanities that had drained him that day. As he spoke, Lucy couldn't help but feel a sense of detachment, as if she were watching a well-rehearsed play unfold. The monotony of his grievances reminded her of the very reasons she had found herself exploring the idea of a different life—a life where her voice and desires mattered more than the endless round of responsibilities they shared. Each word he uttered seemed to echo in her own heart, amplifying her restlessness as she grappled with the monumental decision looming ahead.

Once Johnathon had finished his venting, he turned to Lucy, who sat across from him, her expression a mix of anxiety and boredom. The flickering candlelight casting soft shadows across her face, highlighting the furrow of concern creasing her brow. "What's happened?" he asked, the urgency in his voice rising like the tension in the air.

"Nothing's happened!" Lucy replied, her tone laced with a nervous edge, her fingers nervously fidgeting with the hem of her shirt. But Johnathon could sense something unspoken lingering between them— an invisible weight that pressed down on the conversation.

"Something is wrong, I can feel it!" he insisted, his eyes searching hers for a glimmer of truth. There was a moment of silence, stretched out like an elastic band about to snap, before Lucy finally cracked.

"I'm not happy, Johnathon," she confessed, her voice trembling slightly as if the admission itself was a profound burden. "Our relationship doesn't make me happy anymore. It hasn't for a while if I'm honest." Her gaze shifted to the ground, avoiding the intensity of his stare. "I thought maybe a change of career and a new challenge might shift something in me, but it didn't!"

"What? Since when?" Johnathon's voice was a mixture of disbelief and desperation, each word laden with a sense of urgency to understand.

"Like I said, it's been the case for quite some time now," she continued, her emotions cascading over her like a turbulent wave. "I was scared to tell you in case I was wrong about it, but seeing Trisha and Pablo together only solidified how I've been feeling." She swallowed hard, her eyes glistening as the weight of her words settled between them. "I am sorry!" she added, the apology heavy and sincere.

Johnathon, feeling the ground shift beneath him, began to plead with her, his voice softening. "Please, Lucy, just give me another chance. Let's keep trying. I'll change—just tell me what I need to do to hold onto you." His heart raced as he spoke, hope flickering within him like the dying light of the candle.

Lucy, caught in the tug-of-war between her feelings and his desperate pleas, finally succumbed to the pressure. The walls she had built began to crumble as she started to outline her thoughts, revealing a list of changes that might breathe new life into their faltering relationship. Each suggestion felt like a fragile step towards a future she wasn't sure she wanted, but in that moment, the conversation hung suspended, alive with possibility and unspoken fears.

Over the next couple of months, Johnathon attempted to adjust the way he expressed affection toward Lucy, but his efforts appeared to have insignificant impact on her feelings. Lucy had held onto a glimmer of hope that these changes might reignite something within her, perhaps even a change of heart. However, the more Johnathon tried, the more she found herself drifting away. Instead, she became increasingly attracted to Liam, who had been unwavering in his pursuit of her.

Liam's persistence was refreshing; he consistently reminded her that she deserved someone who would truly appreciate all of her unique qualities. With each conversation, he made her feel seen, valued. Lucy yearned for that kind of attention, the sort that made her feel like the most important person in the world. While she knew that perfection was a fantasy, she found herself daydreaming about a love that made her heart race and her spirit soar.

As the days passed, Lucy finally arranged to go out for a drink with Liam. Excitement coursed through her veins, tinged with anticipation, but for very different reasons than Liam. She was eager for a night of fun and laughter, a welcome distraction from her thoughts, while Liam hoped for a deeper connection that might blossom into something more intimate after their evening out.

On the evening of their outing, Lucy relished the opportunity to dress up. She spent extra time crafting her look, carefully curling the ends of her long, dark hair, allowing it to cascade down her back like a silky waterfall. Her mint green eyes sparkled, enhanced by the dramatic flair of false eyelashes that framed them beautifully.

Donning a sleek black mini dress that clung to her curves with a graceful snugness, Lucy felt empowered and alluring. The fabric shimmered slightly under the soft light of her bedroom, accentuating her figure as she paired it with knee-high black boots that added to her height and confidence. To shield herself from the evening chill, she slipped on a fitted leather jacket, the cool texture perfectly contrasted against the softness of her dress.

As she stood in front of the mirror, ready to step into the night, Lucy caught her reflection and smiled, momentarily forgetting her worries. Tonight was about embracing spontaneity, leaving behind the complexities of her heartache, and perhaps, just perhaps, discovering something new.

Liam's text buzzed on Lucy's phone, breaking the stillness of her house: "Hey you, I'm outside now in the taxi!" As she exchanged warm farewells with Johnathon, a sense of relief washed over her. The confines of the house sometimes felt like a cage, especially in the quiet moments shared only between them. This invitation to step out into the world felt like a breath of fresh air.

As she stepped outside, a cool breeze tousled her hair, and excitement bubbled up within her. Sliding into the backseat of the taxi, Liam's admiring gaze greeted Lucy. The transformation was marked—this wasn't the Lucy known for her crisp shirts and tailored suits at the office; tonight, she wore a black, vibrant mini dress that danced around her. Liam's eyes sparkled with delight as he exclaimed, "Wow! You look amazing!"

"Thanks, you look good yourself!" she replied, a playful smile lighting up her face. The taxi wove through the bustling streets, their laughter punctuating the chatter of the city around them. This short journey felt like an escape; they engaged in a delightful dance of conversation, sharing secrets and vulnerabilities that had remained hidden amid workplace formalities. Each word exchanged deepened their connection, casting aside the usual distractions of their daily lives.

Arriving at the train station, they hurriedly made their way to the queue for the show, all the while animatedly discussing their favourite performances and backstage stories from the theatre. Just as they were about to enter, Lucy's phone buzzed again—this time, it was Jack. She glanced at the screen, the familiar name causing a flicker of uncertainty. Texting back swiftly, she shared that she was out with Liam, anticipating the show.

Jack's response came almost instantaneously, revealing a tinge of disappointment: he wished she had mentioned it earlier. Lucy's fingers flew across the screen as she suggested that perhaps, in the future, he could come to stay in a hotel nearby. "We could drink the mini bar dry and talk about anything and everything," she texted, her heart light with the idea of camaraderie. Jack eagerly replied that he would love that.

The conversation flowed seamlessly, but a small sense of nostalgia lingered in the air. The atmosphere of the venue buzzed with anticipation as the show commenced, a vibrant lineup of comedians ready to take the stage. Lucy and Liam settled into the long, wooden bench, facing each other with an inviting warmth that made the world around them fade away. Laughter bubbled up between them, a joyful response to sharp punchlines and witty observations that danced through the crowd. Each comedian seemed to draw energy from the audience, making playful jabs that elicited roars of laughter and collective groans.

The night unfolded in a blur of humour and camaraderie, punctuated only by brief intermissions when the lights dimmed. During those pauses, Lucy and Liam exchanged glances, the connection deepening with every shared smile. They switched queues for the bar and the restroom with well-orchestrated ease, determined not to lose their hard-won spot among the throngs of fellow patrons.

As the final act bowed to thunderous applause, they stepped out into the brisk October night, the air crisp against their skin. A canopy of stars twinkled overhead, casting a soft glow on the streets filled with laughter and revelry. They meandered toward the nearest bar, their spirits high, only to find themselves amidst a raucous crowd where tipsy revellers stumbled about, their carefree antics not quite resonating with the mood they sought. Discerning the atmosphere wasn't right, they slipped away to another bar, quieter and more intimate.

In a cosy corner, enveloped by low lighting and the gentle hum of conversation, they settled into their seats, drinks in hand. The ambiance shifted into a more personal space, and as they sipped their beverages, their laughter mellowed into the kind of conversation that felt both urgent and soothing.

"Why are you even still with Johnathon?" Liam asked, his brow furrowing slightly in concern. The question hung between them, heavy with unvoiced thoughts. "He clearly doesn't make you happy, and yet you haven't left him. I've known you for almost three years now, and you've never told me anything good he's done for you!" His voice, a mix of frustration and empathy, brought the seriousness of the topic into sharp relief.

Lucy looked down at her drink, swirling the liquid absently, the ice clinking softly against the glass. "I don't know," she sighed, her voice barely above a whisper. "He's been my security blanket for so many years. I guess I'm just scared of leaving him!" The vulnerability in her admission hung in the air, a stark contrast to the laughter that had filled the night just moments before. The warmth of their connection remained, but now it was cloaked in the shadows of doubt and fear, binding them together in a new, yet familiar, way.

The taxi ride home was enveloped in a serene quietness, the gentle sound of the engine blending with the soft rustle of the night outside. The city lights flickered by the window, casting shadows inside the vehicle. As they approached Lucy's house, Liam felt a sense of comfort wash over him. He decided to get out there, the familiar surroundings offering a sense of solace.

Stepping onto the pavement, they shared a lingering hug, a moment filled with warmth as the world around them faded away. Lucy watched as Liam walked away, his figure disappearing into the night.

With a soft sigh, she turned and made her way into the house, the door closing gently behind her.

Inside, the house was quiet, wrapped in the calm of night. Lucy felt the weight of the evening settle over her; it had been a delightful yet exhausting night full of laughter and conversation. She trudged upstairs; her body weary but her heart light. Johnathon was waiting in the bedroom when she arrived, and he attempted to spark a conversation, his voice a soft murmur in the stillness.

However, Lucy could feel her eyelids growing heavy. She offered him a faint smile, her mind already drifting towards the comfort of her bed. "I just need some sleep now," she said, her voice barely above a whisper, conveying a gentle finality. Johnathon nodded understandingly, sensing her fatigue, and he let the conversation fade into silence.

With her heart still softly buzzing from the night, Lucy made her way to the bathroom, where she methodically removed her makeup. Each stroke of the cleansing cloth felt like a release; she peeled away the layers of the evening like shedding armour. After changing into her pyjamas, she padded back to her room, the cool fabric offering a soothing embrace. Sliding beneath the soft covers, she allowed herself to sink into the plush mattress, a sigh escaping her lips as she nestled into the pillows.

Chapter Eight

As Lucy sat at her cluttered desk surrounded by towering stacks of paperwork, the memory of her night out with Liam began to fade like the lingering echoes of laughter. The fluorescent lights above hummed softly, casting a sterile glow over the empty office, amplifying the weight of her solitude. Time had galloped forward over the past couple of weeks; each day bled into the next, leaving her with an overwhelming sense of urgency. She absently tapped her pen against a pile of files, the rhythmic sound a comforting distraction from her thoughts. There had been no word from the elusive Jack—a puzzle she had tried to piece together but ultimately put aside, at least for the moment.

With a week off work looming ahead, Lucy felt a flutter of excitement at the thought of a much-needed break. Although she found fulfilment in her job, each hour spent buried under paperwork had begun to fray the edges of her patience. The anticipation of escape was like a distant beacon, calling to her from the bustling world outside these four walls.

As she meticulously organised her papers, her mind drifted to her colleague, Liam. He had just received the news of his promotion to manager, and a warm feeling of happiness spread through her at the thought. They had shared many work-related banters, and now, being elevated in his career felt significant. Just as she was coming to terms with her thoughts, she heard the old door creak open, the sound echoing like a whisper in the otherwise quiet space.

Suddenly, Liam appeared, his presence filling the void of the empty office. He strode over to her with a confidence that took her by surprise, enveloping her in an unexpected hug. It felt oddly intimate, a stark contrast to their previous interactions. Lucy stiffened for a brief moment, confusion washing over her. Why had he crossed that unspoken line now? They had shared laughter and camaraderie, but this felt different—more personal.

As she returned the embrace hesitantly, her mind raced. Did Liam perceive this shift in their dynamic? A knot of uncertainty tightened in her stomach. She had valued his friendship, even cherished it, but any romantic notions lay firmly outside her purview. She appreciated him, admired him even, but always through the lens of friendship. The way women seemed to gravitate toward him puzzled her; as if they saw a version of Liam that she could never access.

As the hug lingered a heartbeat too long, Lucy's mind began to spiral into a whirlwind of contemplation. The warmth of Liam's embrace wrapped around her, yet it was tinged with uncertainty— would this moment shift the very foundation of their friendship? Or would it evaporate like morning mist, a fleeting misinterpretation she'd have to navigate delicately in the days to come? The gentle hum of the office faded into the background as she wrestled with her thoughts.

"How are you?" Liam asked, his voice breaking the reverie. His familiar smile seemed to hold a hint of curiosity, as if he could sense the turmoil within her.

"I'm good, thanks. How are you?" Lucy responded, forcing a lightness into her tone that belied the weight on her heart.

"Good. Have you spoken to Johnathon yet?" Liam's eyes bore into hers, full of concern and perhaps a touch of impatience.

"Speak to him about what?" she replied, feigning ignorance, though a knot began to tighten in her stomach.

"I assumed after our conversation when we went out that you were going to break up with him?" Liam stated, his brow furrowing slightly, as if he were piecing together an intricate puzzle.

"Why did you assume that?" Lucy shot back, a defensive edge creeping into her voice.

"Because you're not happy, and you even admitted he was just a comfort blanket!" Liam's words were laced with frustration, yet his intent was undeniably genuine.

In that moment, Lucy's heart raced. He was probably right. Deep down, she knew she should have confronted Johnathon about everything that weighed on her, but the reality was that it was none of Liam's business what she and Johnathon discussed or how she felt about her relationship. The truth hung like a heavy shroud: she had already told Johnathon that her feelings hadn't changed, despite his countless efforts to reignite the spark that had long since flickered out. But sharing that detail with Liam felt too vulnerable, too exposing for the confines of their professional relationship.

Choosing her next words carefully, Lucy decided to steer the conversation in a different direction. "Congratulations on your recent promotion!" she exclaimed, injecting a note of sincerity into her voice, hoping to diffuse the tension that lingered in the air like static electricity.

Liam's expression softened, and for a moment, the conversation shifted from the complexities of her personal life to the success he had achieved.

Fortunately, Lucy's week at work whizzed by a sharp contrast to the lingering warmth of her recent hug with Liam. Days blurred together, and before she knew it, the weekend was upon her. She eagerly clocked out, relishing the thought of an entire week dedicated to rest and rejuvenation. On her agenda was a much-anticipated outing with her brother Dale. They had plans to wander through shopping streets, indulging in some retail therapy and sharing a leisurely lunch. The thrill of seeing him again sent a flutter of excitement through her, especially since their conversations had dwindled to quick phone calls lately, leaving her longing for face-to-face interactions.

As the week unfolded, the mundane routine of her job felt like a distant memory, replaced by an exhilarating sense of freedom. The knowledge that she had time to herself was a welcome relief. The emotional distance from Liam also felt oddly comforting. She hadn't heard a word from Jack lately, but she was sure a message would pop up soon; his habit was to reach out every fortnight without fail. Their chats had a familiar rhythm, often revolving around the latest developments in his new relationship, the daily grind of work, and the intriguing details of his mysterious job that always kept her guessing.

Despite enjoying his messages and the curiosity they stirred within her; she realised something had shifted. The thrill of anticipation had dimmed; now, she would wait for his single text with a sense of calm, considering any additional messages a delightful surprise. Lucy felt at peace with this new normal, appreciating the simplicity of their friendship, even though she once harboured hopes of something deep

Lucy found herself spending her weekend with Johnathon, a man who saw their time together as precious moments of connection, while she viewed it as a chore that sapped her energy. The sun had dipped below the horizon, leaving a soft twilight outside, but within her, a discontent had begun to brew. As she sat on the couch, listening to Johnathon talk animatedly about his latest hobby, Lucy's mind wandered to a different place—an imaginary landscape where a tall, handsome stranger would burst through her mundane life and whisk her away to thrilling adventures. Each daydream became more vivid and frequent, shadowing her interactions with Johnathon, whom she respected, but no longer felt any romantic inclination towards. Guilt washed over her like a sudden downpour, realising how unfair it was to harbour such thoughts about a good man.

Finally, the weekend passed like a whisper, and Lucy found herself sitting in her car, parked outside Dale's house, a sigh of relief escaping her lips. The world outside the car was bathed in the soft glow of sunlight, and she could hear the faint rustle of leaves in the breeze. Waiting for Dale felt electric—like the anticipation before a performance. Dale didn't drive, and Lucy was more than happy to pick him up, feeling it an act of love rather than a burden.

Suddenly, there he was—Dale came sashaying up to the car, his confident stride and playful demeanour bringing a smile to her face. He was dressed in a crisp shirt that accentuated his laid-back yet charming personality. As he climbed into the passenger seat beside her, his voice rang with enthusiasm, "Hi gorgeous girl!" The warmth of his greeting wrapped around her like a warm embrace.

"Hey you, you look nice!" she replied, her heart lifting as she took in his easy smile and the way he lit up the space around him.

"As do you! So where are we going?" he asked, his eyes gleaming with excitement, ready for whatever adventure awaited them that day. In that moment, Lucy felt a wave of genuine happiness wash over her, the guilt from her past weekend fading into the background, replaced by the thrill of what was to come.

As they pulled into the bustling car park of the retail park, the sun cast a warm glow over the vibrant storefronts, inviting them to explore. The air buzzed with the lively chatter of other shoppers, and the smell of coffee and freshly cooked food wafted through the entrance of a nearby café. Dale and Lucy stepped out of the car; the excitement of the day ahead evident.

As they navigated through the maze of shops, Dale's jovial spirit took charge. He eagerly filled his arms with an assortment of items—some extravagant, others purely whimsical—that likely would gather dust on his shelf. In contrast, Lucy approached each store with a more cautious eye, her fingers grazing the fabric of clothes and the covers of books, debating whether each item was truly necessary. Their laughter echoed through the aisles as Dale cracked jokes, lightening Lucy's heart, though shadows of her inner thoughts lingered beneath her smile.

After a delightful morning of shopping, treated themselves to lunch at a small restaurant adorned with rustic wooden beams and soft, amber lighting. The tantalizing aroma of herbs and baked bread enveloped them as they entered. Lucy's stomach grumbled, a stark reminder of her recent dieting efforts. She had been meticulously counting calories, trying to shed some pounds, yet her current frame bore no signs of the self-doubt she felt so acutely.

But today, a flicker of resolve sparked within her. Today, she would let go of restriction and simply indulge. As she scanned the menu, her heart raced at the thought of the lasagna—a layered dish she adored, oozing with rich marinara sauce and gooey cheese. A side of cheesy garlic bread would perfectly complement it, the golden, buttery crust promising a delightful crunch. Her mouth watered at the thought, banishing her earlier anxieties.

Dale, ever the sensible one, opted for a prawn salad, vibrant with greens and drizzled in zesty dressing. Nonetheless, he insisted they indulge in dessert, his eyes dancing with mischief as he flipped through the dessert menu, clearly plotting their next sweetness adventure, his playful persistence tugging at Lucy's resolve to be cautious.

Together, they settled into a corner table, the conversation of other diners providing a warm backdrop as they prepared to savour their meals, the sense of camaraderie and shared joy filling them with happiness. Their meal was an absolute delight, a symphony of flavours that danced on their tongues, complemented perfectly by the decadent desserts they savoured and shared afterward. The ambiance of the restaurant was warm and inviting, with low lighting accentuating the bright colours of their plates. Lucy found herself absorbed in conversation with Dale, who was always a source of comfort and wisdom. They discussed Liam's advances, and Dale, with a thoughtful expression, advised her to follow her heart but reminded her of the weighty consequence that came with each choice—once a step was taken, there was no turning back.

Lucy understood the gravity of his words. It was precisely why she had deliberated for so long, weighing her feelings and the implications of her potential decisions. She didn't want to recklessly shatter Johnathon's heart. It had to be a decision grounded in the right reasons, and deep down, she sensed that Liam might not be that right reason. Despite the flirtations and playful exchanges, doubt lingered in her mind.

Throughout the day, as laughter filled the air and the aroma of food enveloped them, Lucy couldn't shake off the sensation of her phone vibrating repeatedly in her pocket. Liam had been texting her, filling the day with thoughts that danced just beneath the surface of her consciousness. Dale found it amusing, chuckling at the stream of messages they exchanged, highlighting the playful banter that unfolded between them.

As they made their way home, paused at traffic lights and surrounded by the glow of daylight, Lucy's phone chimed again. She instinctively glanced at the screen, expecting to see Liam's name flash across it, but to her surprise, it was Jack instead. His message detailed his new girlfriend, a whirlwind of excitement laced with the complexity of her having a child. Lucy, always mindful and responsible, offered her advice cautiously. She reminded him of the delicate nature of relationships involving children—how when hearts break, it's not just the adults who suffer; the child carries the burden too.

To her astonishment, Jack responded almost instantaneously, his words a mix of agreement and revelation. "You're right," he typed back, after she had revealed that she, too, was contemplating ending things with Johnathon. Lucy felt a rush of confusion at his response. What could it mean?

"He likes you!" Dale chimed in, his eyes sparkling with mischief as he leaned back in his seat.

"Don't be ridiculous! He's, my friend; we don't have that sort of relationship!" Lucy shot back, her voice a mixture of denial and apprehension. Dale rolled his eyes, a gesture familiar between them, as he pressed on, "I'm telling you, he likes you!" His certainty hung in the air, challenging Lucy to reconsider the possibility blooming just beneath the surface of their friendship.

Lucy dropped Dale off at his doorstep, the afternoon air cool and crisp as the last light of day was starting to fade into twilight. They exchanged warm goodbyes, lingering for a moment longer as if reluctant to part ways. As she drove away, thoughts of Jack flickered in her mind, igniting a sense of curiosity she hadn't felt in ages.

Her phone buzzed with a flurry of notifications, breaking the comfortable silence of her car. Messages continued to flow between Lucy and Jack, an unexpected surge of communication that both surprised and thrilled her. This was not like Jack; he was typically reserved, sending only a few messages here and there. But tonight, each of her texts seemed to spark something in him. With every reply, a little flicker of hope ignited in her heart, a feeling that perhaps he was finally opening up.

Jack's tone felt different too, more engaged and animated. It was as if the revelation of her intentions to leave Johnathon had lifted a veil between them, allowing him to connect with her in a way he hadn't before. His responses came quickly, and as the conversation flowed effortlessly into the night, Lucy found herself captivated, lost in the delightful exchange.

At some point, the laughter softened, the chat winding down as Jack mentioned he needed to get some rest for work in the morning. His last message lingered in the air, "You're really easy to talk to, and I've enjoyed our conversation." Those simple words wrapped around Lucy like a warm blanket on a chilly night, stirring emotions within her that had lain dormant for far too long.

As she settled into bed, the room cloaked in darkness, a rush of excitement coursed through her veins. The anticipation felt thrilling, almost intoxicating. It had been ages since she felt so hopeful about the possibility of something new. Was her tall, handsome stranger finally stepping out from the shadows? She couldn't help but smile, her heart fluttering with the promise of what could be.

As the morning light filtered through her window, Lucy stirred from her sleep, her mind immediately flickering to thoughts of Jack. She found herself pondering whether she would face yet another long, two-week silence without a message from him, as had become his routine. The clock ticked softly, and she could feel a mixture of hope and anxiety knotting in her stomach.

It didn't take long for her anticipation to bear fruit. Suddenly, her phone chimed, breaking the quiet of her room with a familiar sound that sent a thrill down her spine. It was a message from Jack, but this one felt different; there was an unmistakable hint of flirtation woven into his words. As her eyes scanned the text, she noted the playful tone and the surprising addition of an 'x' at the end—a small gesture that made her heart race. It was as if Dale's teasing suggestion that Jack harboured deeper feelings for her was finally being validated.

Eager to keep the momentum going but wanting to maintain a veneer of casualness, Lucy quickly typed out a reply, carefully keeping her tone neutral as she enquired about his work. Yet, her heart raced as she hit send, each second feeling like an eternity. Jack's response came almost immediately, warm and animated, as he regaled her with amusing tales from the office, interspersed with subtle, flirtatious remarks that sent butterflies swirling in her stomach.

Her heart skipped a beat—this was the connection she had longed for since the moment their texting began, a desire she had buried under layers of doubt and resignation. Jack's subsequent revelation that he had ended his relationship with his girlfriend sent a jolt through Lucy. Was this a door opening? A flicker of hope ignited within her, but she was apprehensive. Jack reassured her, gently acknowledging the complexity of her own relationship with Johnathon, understanding the weight of shared years and a home woven together.

As days turned into weeks, their texts morphed into a dance of flirtation and adoration, each message becoming more intimate, drawing them closer together. They began exchanging whispers of what they meant to each other, dreams of a potential future that felt tantalisingly within reach.

Amid the excitement, Lucy felt a familiar wave of responsibility wash over her—a nagging guilt that settled heavily in her chest. She knew the time had come to confront Johnathon. It wouldn't be fair to continue this blossoming relationship with Jack without first untangling the life she had built with Johnathon. The thought of the coming conversation loomed over her, a bittersweet reminder of the choices she had to make as her heart raced toward a new possibility.

Chapter Nine

Lucy sat in the dimly lit living room, the flickering flames of the fireplace casting shadows upon the walls and dancing across her anxious face. The rich aroma of the dinner she had prepared lingered in the air—a comforting blend of herbs and spices intended to create an inviting atmosphere. She had envisioned this evening as the moment she would finally discuss the weighty decision she had been carrying in her heart, the decision to end her relationship with Johnathon.

Outside, the December chill wrapped around the house, the world draped in darkness, but inside, Lucy's mind was racing. She could still hear Jack's reassuring voice echoing in her ears, telling her that there was no rush to decide; he would wait as long as necessary because she meant everything to him. Yet, an undeniable urge told her that tonight was right.

As the minutes stretched into hours, her anticipation mingled with irritation. Johnathon was late—too late. Finally, a dull chime from her phone broke the silence, and she felt her heart sink. A text from him lit up the screen: he was working late. Lucy's frustration simmered just below the surface. She quickly typed a response, her fingers moving with purpose but laden with annoyance. She needed to speak with him urgently, and yet here he was, staying away.

His reply pierced through her resolve, a question that resonated deeply: Was this it? Was she really breaking up with him? She read his words with a mix of sadness and anger, feeling the weight of their shared past loom over her. He offered to go to his parents' house, inadvertently granting her the very escape she sought. Deep down, she could sense his hope hanging in the air, a silent plea for her to say she wanted him, that everything could be different. But with a heavy heart, she typed back, urging him to go, punctuating her message with an apology that felt inadequate but necessary.

As soon as she hit send, an overwhelming sense of relief washed over her like a warm tide. It felt as if a suffocating weight had lifted from her shoulders, the kind that had been pressing down on her for months, maybe years. No longer would she find herself immersed in the turmoil of secret texts or purposeless drives through the empty streets, compelled to hide her true feelings.

Now, she could finally breathe, releasing the tension that had tangled her thoughts and emotions. The flicker of hope reignited within her—a vision of a future that included Jack, one filled with honesty and the promise of genuine connection.

Instantly, a flutter of anxiety coursed through Lucy as she typed out a message to Jack, her fingers dancing over the screen, hoping for a reply that would reassure her she had made the right decision. The glow from her phone illuminated her face in the dim light of her room, casting shadows that mirrored her uncertainty. But when the night grew quiet and Jack didn't respond, she was left alone with her thoughts, replaying her choices like a film on repeat.

The first light of dawn broke in the morning, bringing with it a tinge of hope. When Jack finally reached out, his message was gentle yet probing, asking why she had chosen that moment to end things. With careful words, Lucy laid bare the emotional turmoil she had endured, explaining what had led her to this pivotal choice. Jack's responses were warm and comforting, and there was a genuine note of happiness in his words that resonated with her. Still, beneath the surface of his messages, Lucy detected a hint of uncertainty, a flicker of doubt.

Deep in her heart, Lucy was aware that she had made the right choice, even if it meant facing the prospect of solitude. Keeping Johnathon in a loveless relationship was unfair to both of them, a truth she couldn't ignore. Her decision felt empowering, as if she were reclaiming her own narrative—not just choosing Jack over Johnathon but choosing herself first.

As the days unfolded, Lucy and Jack's conversations blossomed into something tender and affectionate. Plans began to take shape for Jack's visit to her home in the new year, a thrilling prospect that sent butterflies flocking to her stomach. Two years had slipped away since they last met, yet the feelings she harboured for him felt as vibrant and urgent as ever.

As Christmas approached, a warm glow of excitement enveloped Lucy, illuminating her new life. She immersed herself in precious moments spent with her brother and parents, relishing the laughter and love that filled their homes. Yet, in the quiet hours, she cherished her solitude, finding comfort in Jack's regular messages that punctuated her days. Though Jack was busy with work over the Christmas period, they filled the void with phone calls and texts, weaving a tapestry of connection, each conversation a thread binding them closer together. They had resigned themselves to the reality of not seeing each other until January 2nd, but that anticipation only heightened her excitement, making each day feel like a step closer to something beautiful.

Lucy woke up on Christmas morning, the soft golden light of dawn streaming through the curtains and casting a warm glow in her bedroom. The scent of pine from the tree she had decorated lingered in the air. Excitement bubbled within her as she quickly grabbed her phone and typed a heartfelt message to Jack, wishing him a very merry Christmas. She wanted him to know that he was the first person to occupy her thoughts on this magical morning.

By the time the clock ticked toward the afternoon, she felt a flutter of anticipation when her phone buzzed with a response. Jack's message was filled with positivity and joy, even though he was at work, making her heart race. They exchanged texts throughout the day, their playful banter punctuated by laughter. Later that evening, they had an extraordinarily long phone conversation, each word drawing them even closer. The hours seemed to fly by as they talked about everything and anything, wrapped in the warmth of their connection. Lucy didn't have to work the next day, but Jack did, so they reluctantly ended their call around 4 a.m., knowing he needed some rest.

As she lay in bed, her mind danced with a world of possibilities. A giddy rush of happiness coursed through her; she marvelled that she could feel this alive and invigorated. Jack had stirred something in her soul that felt like a fresh breeze sweeping through her life, and she savoured every moment of their new romance. The memories of her past drama with Liam faded into oblivion, a distant echo she had long since forgotten.

On Boxing Day, Lucy rose early, the sun spilling into her kitchen as she decided to prepare a special meal for her brother, Dale. It had been ages since he had visited her, and she was eager to welcome him into her home. With newfound energy, she began cooking, instinctively reaching for the ingredients as if they were old friends. Lucy meticulously basted a golden-brown chicken, covering it generously with fragrant herbs and minced garlic. She filled the pans with a colourful array of vegetables, their vibrant colours promising a feast that would tantalize the taste buds. To complement the meal, she carefully prepared Yorkshire puddings, their batter bubbling with potential.

With everything ready, all she needed now was to fetch Dale. Anticipation fluttered in her chest as she grabbed her coat and headed to pick him up. On the way, she sent Jack a voice note, excitedly telling him about her plans for the day. His response came back, strangely vague, as he mentioned he might have to go away that night but promised to keep her updated. Curiosity piqued, Lucy replied, enquiring about where he might have to go, but her message lingered unanswered. She shrugged it off, assuming he was preoccupied with work, and focused instead on making the most of her time with Dale.

Days slipped by like grains of sand, each moment stretching into a lingering silence as Jack's absence loomed ever larger in Lucy's mind. With each message she sent bathed in hope, the harsh reality of undelivered notifications gnawed at her insides, sparking a whirlwind of anxiety. What if something had happened to him? The gnawing thought that she might never know the truth consumed her. No one else was privy to their secret connection, so who would inform her of his fate?

As New Year's Eve approached, an unsettling sense of loneliness wrapped around her heart like a heavy weight. In a moment of yearning for companionship, Lucy invited her childhood friend Mia over for a drink. She shuffled through the muted glow of her home, which felt unusually empty without Jack's lively presence and the warmth of their long conversations.

When Mia arrived, with her petite frame standing at only five feet tall, she brought a rush of familiarity into the room. Her shoulder-length blonde hair was pulled back in a messy bun, a testament to their unwritten rule of comfort over glamour. Dressed in soft tracksuit bottoms and a cosy oversized sweater, Mia embodied the relaxed spirit they both sought that evening.

They settled into the plush, worn-out couch, surrounded by flickering fairy lights that cast a warm golden glow, almost masking the sorrow that lingered in the air. As they poured glasses of wine, the rich, deep crimson liquid swirled like a dance between their hopes and fears, each sip prompting Lucy to spill her thoughts about Jack's disappearance. Mia listened intently, her mahogany brown eyes wide with concern, the warmth in her voice both soothing and grounding.

"What if his phone is broken? It's possible he couldn't afford a new one right now, especially with-it being Christmas" Mia suggested, her voice gentle. "Or maybe he had to leave on one of those mysterious jobs he mentioned?"

Lucy's heart sank further at the thought, each possibility distilling her hope into a cocktail of sadness. As the clock inched toward midnight, a pang of desolation washed over her. The noise of celebration from outside felt painfully distant, and despite the festive atmosphere, she felt adrift in a sea of uncertainty.

Yet, as the countdown approached, the pair found joy in their shared laughter and memories, losing themselves in the moment. Together, they toasted to new beginnings, attempting to drown out the aching void Jack's absence had carved into the night. They revelled in the intoxication, but beneath the surface, Lucy's heart still ached with the question that lingered: where was Jack? As the clock struck midnight, casting a silvery glow over the room, Lucy found herself seated at her cluttered kitchen table, illuminated by the soft light of her laptop. With a slight wobble from the wine she had consumed, she composed an email to Jack, hoping to convey her warm wishes for a happy new year. Determined to reach out, she figured that if her messages weren't getting through, perhaps an email would do the trick.

The night wore on, and as the early morning hours faded away, Mia finally decided to call it a night, leaving Lucy to grapple with the effects of a little too much alcohol. It was around 5am when Lucy staggered to her bedroom, feeling the weight of the alcohol crash over her. She slipped under the covers, oblivious to the world around her, and soon fell into a restless sleep that the night's revelries had permitted.

Hours later, on New Year's Day, Lucy lazily opened her laptop, blinking against the bright screen, and logged into her email. To her surprise, there was a message waiting for her—a reply from Jack. Her heart skipped a beat as she clicked it open. Jack's words flowed over the screen, each line filled with sincerity and a torrent of emotions he hadn't fully expressed before. He wished her a joyful start to the new year, but it was the subsequent words that sent a shiver down her spine.

Before he had disappeared from her life, Jack had confessed his love for her, a revelation lingering in the air like a sweet fragrance. In the haze of her drunken stupor, Lucy realised she had reciprocated those feelings, declaring her love for him in an impassioned, momentary lapse of inhibition. Yet, as she read his heartfelt response, a wave of confusion washed over her. She couldn't quite recall writing such a declaration, nor was she entirely sure if it was genuine. Lucy felt a stirring deep within her—a new and confusing kind of affection for Jack that seemed to surpass what she had felt before. But whether it was true love or merely a reflection of the night's intoxicated bravado remained a mystery that lingered in her mind. Jack had mentioned in his email, the words spilling out like a torrent of grief, that he had been whisked away on urgent business for his other employer. Yet, within that whirlwind of responsibilities, he had been granted a precious day to attend the funeral of his beloved sister, who had sadly passed away before he left.

While their conversations had touched on his struggles, Lucy knew little about Jack's family background. It wasn't until he revealed that his sister had been hospitalised that she learned of her existence. Jack had dedicated countless days and sleepless nights at her bedside, bearing silent witness to her battle until the inevitable came to claim her. After nearly a month of waiting, the sombre day of her funeral had finally arrived, landing cruelly on the 2nd of January—a date that now felt like an anchor in Lucy's mind, pulling her thoughts into a mix of mourning and concern. She realised, with a heavy heart, that he wouldn't be able to keep his promise to visit her.

Understanding his sorrow, Lucy could only imagine the gravity of the situation. Not only was he entangled in his demanding job, but he was also facing one of life's most harrowing challenges: saying goodbye to a loved one. She longed to know the location of the funeral, wishing she could quietly appear to offer her support, to wrap him in a comforting embrace during his time of need.

Days crawled by, each one stretching into an eternity without any word from Jack. The silence between them felt palpable. Despite her worry, Lucy decided to send messages—each one a thread of connection that lay waiting for him, like a lifeline he could grasp when he returned.

Then, nearly a week later, while she was immersed in her work, her phone suddenly pinged, cutting through the mundane routine like a bolt of lightning. It was Jack. As she opened the message, she was pulled into the painful, poignant narrative he wove about his experiences at the funeral—the emotional currents and heart-wrenching trials he'd faced at work. Each word painted a vivid picture of his turmoil, and she could hear the tremor in his voice through the text.

Her concern for his welfare surged a wave of fear crashing against the rocky shoreline of her heart. Yet amidst the shadows of worry, an unexpected spark of excitement flickered to life within her. It was a strange juxtaposition, feeling a rush of adrenaline as she read about his dangerous encounters. The combination of fear for his safety and an undeniable thrill at his experiences created a whirlwind of emotions that both confused and energised her as she processed everything he shared. Amidst all of this though Lucy felt a sense of relief that they could finally get back to normal.

A couple of weeks passed, and with them returned the comforting rhythm of Lucy and Jack's late-night conversations that flowed into the early hours, coupled with their playful daytime messaging. The familiarity of their exchanges brought a wave of relief to Lucy's heart. Jack had mentioned, almost offhandedly, that he would need to travel abroad to the Middle East at some undefined point in the future, a thought that filled her with trepidation. The uncertainty of his safety gnawed at her, and she found herself secretly wishing that the trip would somehow be cancelled or delayed.

One crisp Saturday morning, Lucy was jolted awake by the insistent ring of her phone. Squinting against the morning light, she could barely recall her late-night conversation with Jack, who had mentioned he was driving to see a family member in another part of the country. As she rubbed the sleep from her eyes, her gaze fell on the screen, which was flashing with Jack's name. A voice note chimed in, and she listened to his warm, affectionate words wishing her a peaceful sleep.

Still groggy, she typed a quick response, letting him know that she was awake now. Almost instantaneously, another voice note pinged in. "Lucy, is your bedroom front facing or rear facing?" he asked, a hint of mischief lacing his voice. Feeling slightly puzzled by the question, she replied, "Front facing."

Then, her phone buzzed again. "Look out of your window," he instructed, his tone playful yet urgent.

A thrill of anticipation coursed through her as she peered outside. There he stood, a striking figure on her driveway, leaning casually against the front gate. The early morning sun illuminated his chiselled features and accentuated the strength of his broad shoulders. He looked utterly captivating, a vision of confidence and charm right outside her house, making her heart race as she took in the sight of him. Lucy hurried down the stairs. With a sudden burst of excitement, she flung open the door, revealing Jack standing on the other side, his expression a mix of surprise and joy. As their eyes locked, an electric warmth surged between them, and without hesitation, they rushed into each other's arms. The embrace was tight and sincere, wrapping them in a cocoon of comfort, making time feel irrelevant as they relished the moment.

Chapter Ten

Lucy opened the door wider, her heart fluttering with a mix of surprise and joy as she welcomed Jack into her small yet cosy living room. The early morning sunlight filtered through the curtains, casting a warm glow around the room. She could still smell the faint scent of coffee wafting from her kitchen from the night before, and as she busied herself brewing a fresh cup, she couldn't help but think about the long drive he had endured just to be here. The thought of Jack's determination added to the thrill of his unexpected visit.

She turned to him, noticing the way his perfectly shaven head caught the light and the twinkle in his eyes. He shared how he had driven through the night, navigating lonely motorways and desolate stretches of road, with only the sounds of the engine and the occasional snippet of the radio to keep him company. "I didn't want to wake you," he explained, a hint of sheepishness in his smile. "I thought it'd be best to wait until morning."

Lucy couldn't believe he'd been parked outside her house, sending her messages that had gone unanswered. She felt a rush of affection as she thought about how he had been patient, confirming her deep slumber with every passing minute. It wasn't until around 7am that she finally roused from her sleep and spotted his messages, her heart skipping a beat at the realisation that he was just outside.

As they settled onto the sofa, the world outside seemed to fade away. Their laughter echoed in the air, punctuating the comfortable silence as they exchanged stories, recalling their last meeting that felt like both ages ago and yet just yesterday. Lucy could feel an invisible thread pulling them closer, drawing them together like magnets in the tranquillity of the moment.

Wrapped in a soft blanket, they cuddled, the warmth and closeness intensifying the electric connection between them.

After a while, Lucy's practical side kicked in; she had a few errands to run. Jack's face lit up when she mentioned it. "Can I drive you?" he asked with genuine excitement. There was something sweetly chivalrous about his eagerness, especially as Lucy had revealed in their previous chats how she longed for someone to chauffeur her now and then—how the idea of being driven around appealed to her sense of adventure.

"Absolutely!" she replied, her enthusiasm matching his as they made their way to the door, ready to embrace the day together, the promise of more shared moments ahead hanging in the air like a delicious secret.

As Lucy and Jack wandered through the aisles of the bustling DIY store, the scent of fresh paint and polished wood filled the air, mingling with the excitement of potential transformation. After Johnathon's abrupt departure, Lucy had thrown herself into making changes to their once-shared home, her heart a mix of nostalgia and determination.

She was slowly sifting through the remnants of Johnathon's belongings, packing them with care over time, each item holding a memory—some sweet, some bitter. As she navigated through the store, a sense of relief washed over her, knowing she had Jack by her side, ready to lend a hand. His presence was like a warm, reassuring light, illuminating the path ahead of her.

"I can't wait to tackle those projects together," Jack enthused, his eyes sparkling with genuine enthusiasm. His promise of teamwork felt like an invigorating breath of fresh air, a stark contrast to her previous experiences. Lucy's heart fluttered at the thought; she had long yearned for a partnership where they could build and create together, and this felt like the beginning of something beautiful.

They decided to take a break, slipping into a small café tucked away in the corner of the store. The rich aroma of freshly brewed coffee surrounded them as they settled into comfortable chairs, distant voices and laughter providing a familiar backdrop. Jack leaned in, his voice filled with a mix of excitement and concern, as he shared news of his upcoming work trip to the Middle East.

"It looks like it's going to be March now," he said, his brows furrowing slightly. Yet, as Lucy listened, she felt a flicker of hope—March seemed far enough away, offering them precious weeks to explore each other's lives a little more deeply before he set off on his journey. The thought of spending those upcoming weeks together ignited a sense of joy within her.

As they sipped their coffee, the conversation flowed effortlessly, punctuated by laughter and shared glances that spoke volumes. In that moment, surrounded by the lively atmosphere of the café and the promise of new beginnings, Lucy could almost envision a brighter future blossoming—a future built on the foundations of trust, support, and genuine connection.

When they returned to the house, the air was filled with a sense of accomplishment as they completed their DIY tasks together. Laughter and playful banter echoed around them, mingling with the smell of fresh paint and sawdust. As the sun dipped below the horizon, casting the remnants of the afternoon sun through the windows, they settled down on the couch, wrapped in a knitted blanket, ready to enjoy a well-deserved evening of television.

It was in this intimate setting, with the soft glow of the screen illuminating their faces, that they finally shared their first kiss. It was slow, tender, and suspended in time—a short, lingering moment that sent delightful shivers down Lucy's spine. Her heart raced, and a blissful smile spread across her face, lighting up her features. It felt as though every moment that had led to this had culminated in the best day she had ever experienced.

As they cuddled under the blanket, their hands roamed gently across each other's bodies, exploring and familiarising themselves with every curve and contour. Lucy's fingers brushed over the myriads of scars that adorned Jack's skin. Each scar told a story, a testament to battles fought and lessons learned. She admired the ruggedness they represented, even as Jack seemed self-conscious under her gaze.

"Scars are markers of a life lived," she told him softly, her voice full of warmth and understanding. Jack looked at her, his eyes searching for reassurance as she traced a particularly prominent scar on his side. It fascinated her—the way it felt beneath her fingertips, the way it added depth to him. Resting her head against his chest, she stroked it gently, feeling the rhythm of his heartbeat in tandem with her own.

As the hours melted away, lost in each other's presence, Jack finally broke the spell. He reluctantly mentioned that he had to drive back home for work the next morning. Lucy's heart sank at the thought of their evening coming to an end. A soft frown creased her brow, disappointment threading through her tone. She understood the necessity of his departure yet wished for the warmth of his company to linger just a little longer.

Jack noticed her expression, and with a gentle squeeze of her hand, he reassured her. "I promise I'll be back soon. Next time, I'll book a hotel, just for us," he said, a spark of excitement in his eyes. Lucy sat up slightly, curiosity piqued. She confessed that she had only ever stayed in hotels abroad, on holiday adventures, and the prospect of experiencing a British hotel with him filled her with giddy anticipation.

They shared a knowing smile, the promise of future moments sparking between them like electricity, wrapping them in a cocoon of hope and tender longing as the night deepened around them.

Back in the bustling office on Monday, Lucy felt an electrifying spring in her step, the kind that came with the thrill of a newfound romance. The flurry of emotions bubbled within her, excitement swirling alongside a subtle yet unsettling hint of anxiety regarding Jack's upcoming trip to the Middle East. His vague comments about the journey hung in the air like an unsung melody, leaving her with an ache of curiosity that she couldn't quite shake. Jack had a knack for keeping certain aspects of his life shrouded in mystery, but for reasons beyond her comprehension, Lucy found herself accepting his evasiveness. Deep down, she desired for things to blossom between them, and her heart yearned for it so fiercely that she was willing to overlook the shadows of doubt.

Smitten didn't begin to cover what Lucy felt for Jack; it was as if he had cast a spell over her. She was inexplicably drawn to him, captivated by the way his laughter danced through the air and the glint in his eyes that hinted at hidden depths. Each passing day felt imbued with a sense of longing, and she often caught herself pondering whether her heartfelt declaration of love in that email was a fleeting moment of impulse or a genuine reflection of her feelings.

As she settled into her desk, the familiar sounds of office life bustling around her, Lucy heard the sound of Liam's voice slicing through the chatter. He sauntered into the office with an air of confidence, his gaze locking onto her as he approached. Without hesitation, he began to flirt, his tone laced with charm. However, to Lucy, it felt hollow and uninviting. With a gentle shake of her head, she brushed aside his advances, escaping the office for her daily commitments. In her heart, she knew exactly who she wanted, and it was certainly not Liam—the thought of him was merely background noise in the symphony of her emotions for Jack.

As she moved through her daily visits, her mind remained a whirlwind, preoccupied with memories of the enchanting weekend that had felt as though it had been woven just for them. Each moment spent with Jack had been a treasure, leaving her with a profound sense of joy that she wished she could stretch into eternity. It was as if every second spent in his company was an elixir, intoxicating and utterly addictive, and she found herself craving more of him, desperately wanting to entwine their lives together, wrapped in the magic they created together. In those fleeting hours, Lucy realised she would happily lose herself in him forever, each heartbeat echoing the thrill of their relationship.

Lucy and Jack spoke every day, their voices weaving a comforting thread of connection that filled the silence of their lives. Each conversation was an escape, with Lucy finding herself spellbound by Jack's deep southern tones, rich and melodic, each word dripping with charm. As they chatted for hours, Lucy couldn't help but envision their future together—a vivid tale of laughter, love, and shared moments. Their bond grew stronger with each passing week, blossoming like fresh spring flowers.

One evening, as the sun dipped below the horizon, Jack revealed exciting news: he had booked a hotel for the upcoming weekend, a getaway just for the two of them. Lucy felt a rush of elation coursing through her veins; the thought of spending a whole weekend with him felt like a dream coming true. The days that followed dragged on agonisingly, each hour stretching into an eternity as she counted down the moments until they could be together again.

As Friday approached, the anticipation became nearly unbearable. Jack called her in the evening, his voice full of warmth and excitement, letting her know he was en route. Her heart raced; she could almost feel the energy of his presence through the phone. Rushing home, Lucy was a whirlwind of activity as she prepared for his arrival. She treated her hair with care, letting soft waves cascade down her back, framing her face beautifully.

Choosing the perfect outfit felt like a monumental task, but she ultimately selected a short black skort that hugged her curves just right, paired with sleek black heels that added a hint of drama to her look. With a silky orange halter neck top, she felt vibrant and confident, the colour echoing her excitement. As she misted herself with her favourite perfume—a delicate blend of floral and vanilla—she couldn't help but smile at her reflection, feeling fabulous and ready for the evening ahead.

Just as she finalised her packing, a sharp knock broke through her reverie. Lucy squealed with delight, her heart fluttering as she rushed to the door. Opening it wide, she was met with the sight of Jack standing tall and handsome on her doorstep. His broad shoulders and charming smile made her breath hitch momentarily. "Wow, you look absolutely beautiful!" he exclaimed, his eyes sparkling with admiration. In that moment, Lucy felt cherished, and she couldn't wait for the weekend to unfold.

They decided to spend some quality time together at Lucy's home before setting off to the hotel, which was only a couple of miles away.

Jack had suggested this little getaway because he wanted to give Lucy the experience of a hotel stay in the UK—as she had confided to him she had never done this before. As they settled into the car, excitement bubbled within Lucy, but it was tinged with an undercurrent of nervousness. She felt a flutter in her stomach, wondering if she truly knew Jack well enough to share a hotel room with him. However, she quickly dismissed the thought; turning down the opportunity to deepen their connection seemed unthinkable. With her house in disarray—a chaotic canvas of memories from her past, particularly in the wake of clearing out Johnathon's belongings—she found the idea of a tidy hotel room immensely appealing.

As they drove through the streets, wrapped in the glow of the late afternoon sun, their conversation flowed easily. They laughed and reminisced about their time spent together, exchanging stories filled with warmth and laughter. The ambiance was light, yet beneath it, there was an unspoken tension as they both anticipated the unknown that lay ahead. They had become incredibly close during Jack's last visit, sharing soft whispers and fleeting touches as their fingers grazed each other's skin, their intimacy still lying on the brink of exploration. The thought of sharing a bed made Lucy's heart race; it felt like a significant leap into deeper intimacy.

While Jack openly expressed his love for Lucy, telling her regularly just how much she meant to him, she felt a mixture of joy and apprehension at his words. She had told him she loved him once, sparked by emotions she had struggled to acknowledge fully. Now, as they approached the hotel, the weight of the moment pressed heavily on her—a mix of thrill and fear swirled within her. Would this be a natural progression for them, or would it change everything? Lucy took a deep breath, determined to embrace the unfolding adventure, knowing that sometimes, the most beautiful moments in life come from stepping into the unknown.

They checked into the hotel, fingers interlaced, as they made their way through the expansive, elegantly decorated lobby. The space was adorned with plush velvet furniture, glittering chandeliers, and art pieces that whispered stories of sophistication and luxury. Lucy couldn't believe that this was the kind of place Jack was accustomed to. It was a far cry from the quaint B&Bs she had envisioned for the UK. The realisation struck her like a bolt of lightning—Jack must spend a considerable amount of time in hotels, especially when she noticed the gleaming loyalty card for the hotel chain nestled in his wallet.

As they approached their room, Jack paused to unlock the door, his smile widening as he gestured for Lucy to enter first. With a soft click, the door swung open, revealing a breathtaking suite. The room was spacious, bathed in warm, golden light that spilled in through large windows draped with sumptuous curtains. Rich, earthy tones adorned the walls, complemented by tasteful artwork and stylish furnishings that exuded comfort and class.

"So, what do you think?" Jack asked, his voice filled with genuine excitement after shutting the door behind them. Lucy stepped inside, her eyes widening in delight. "It's beautiful!" she exclaimed, taking in the plush king-sized bed with an inviting array of pillows, the sleek wooden surfaces, and the plush area rug that softened the room's ambiance.

Jack beamed at her reaction, nodding earnestly. He shared that he always chooses to stay with this particular hotel chain, as their rooms were consistently the nicest, he had encountered, even if they came with a slightly higher price tag. Lucy couldn't help but feel a rush of envy mixed with admiration; it was clear that Jack had a taste for the finer things in life, and now she was part of this world, if only for a fleeting moment. Lucy felt an overwhelming sense of warmth and affection wash over her, knowing that Jack had gone out of his way to create this moment just for her. She kicked off her shoes, the soft fabric of the carpet welcoming her bare feet and took a deep breath to steady her nerves as she climbed onto the bed. Jack reclined there, surrounded by a mountain of plush pillows that framed his figure, making him look both relaxed and inviting.

As she settled beside him, he instinctively pulled her close, wrapping his arms around her with a comforting strength. "I've missed this!" he exclaimed, his voice a mix of joy and longing as he hugged her tightly, enveloping her in his warmth. Lucy felt her heart swell at the sincerity of his words. "Me too!" she replied, her voice a gentle whisper filled with uncontainable emotion.

They lay there together, caught in a timeless embrace that felt both fleeting and infinite, as if the world outside had ceased to exist. Every moment of separation vanished, replaced by the familiar rhythm of each other's heartbeat. It felt as though they had been separated by invisible chains of circumstance, each nursing the scars of their time apart.

Jack's gaze softened as he looked down at Lucy, his eyes reflecting a myriad of unspoken feelings. With a tender touch, he lifted her chin with his index finger, coaxing her to meet his gaze. The moment froze, their breaths mingling in the air as they lost themselves in each other's eyes, the space between them charged with an electric mix of affection and understanding. Just then, he leaned in close, the warmth of his body enveloping her, and planted the most passionate kiss Lucy had ever experienced on her lips. It was as if time stood still; her heart raced as her senses heightened. The kiss was electric, sparking a tingling sensation that spread from her lips through her entire body, sending delightful shivers cascading down her spine. She could taste the sweetness of the moment and feel the intensity of his emotions pouring into her, igniting a fire deep within her. For an instant, nothing else mattered; they were lost in a world of their own, a whirlwind of longing and connection that left her breathless. Their bodies intertwined, skin brushing against skin, as they sank deeper into each other's warmth. The night hung heavy with electricity, crackling in the air around them like a sudden summer storm. Every shared breath felt like a whispered secret, heightening the intensity of their connection. They lost track of time, the moonlight casting a silvery glow that danced softly across their features, illuminating the passion in their eyes and bodies. As they pressed closer, lost in a whirlwind of emotions, they felt breathless and utterly spent, as if the world had faded away, leaving just the two of them enveloped in an exquisite stillness. The pair slept soundly for the rest of the night, cocooned in the warmth of each other's arms, until rays of the morning sun began to filter through the curtains, signalling almost lunchtime the following day. Having exhausted every last morsel of energy on their nighttime escapades, they found themselves enveloped in a euphoric haze, basking in the bliss of the morning after.

Lucy was the first to rouse, her eyes fluttering open to the soft, golden light that danced across the sheets. She stretched languidly, savouring the comfort of the moment, and then quietly slipped out of bed, careful not to disturb Jack. He had driven for hours the day before, and she knew he could use a bit more rest.

As she made her way to the bathroom, the coolness of the tiled floor sent a delightful shiver up her spine. The bathroom was filled with the soothing sounds of water, and as she stepped into the shower, she revelled in the warmth cascading over her. She worked her fingers through her hair, trying her best to keep the noise to a minimum, enjoying the blissful solitude of the moment.

Just as she began to rinse the lather from her hair, she felt a sudden rush of air and a playful tug at the shower curtain. It was swiftly pulled back, and there stood Jack, a cheeky grin spreading across his face. In all his glory, he stood illuminated by the diffused light of the bathroom, a playful sparkle in his eyes that promised mischief. The unexpected sight sent a thrill through Lucy, turning her peaceful morning into a delightful surprise filled with laughter, love and unexpected intimacy.

After their warm, soothing shower, they emerged wrapped in fluffy towels, the gentle steam still clinging to the air like a nostalgic embrace. Hours melted away as they settled into the plush cocoon of their hotel room, entwined in each other's arms on the soft, inviting bed creating many more intimate memories. The flickering glow of the television lit the room with a soft, golden haze, casting gentle shadows that danced along the walls, creating an atmosphere of tranquillity. They didn't feel the need for constant conversation; the silence was filled with the unspoken magic of their connection, a comfortable rhythm of companionship that spoke more than words ever could.

As the hours slipped by, time seemed inconsequential. They cherished the rare solitude, sharing soft laughter and stolen glances, their hearts harmonising in a beautiful symphony of intimacy. With each moment, they discovered layers of closeness that ignited an exhilarating blend of pleasure and excitement within them. Every gentle touch and kiss solidified their bond, as if their bodies were perfectly in tune, resonating with an energy that neither of them had ever experienced before. The thrill of their connection sent electric currents coursing through their veins, making them feel alive in a way that was utterly intoxicating. This blissful weekend was unfolding into a tapestry of intimate moments, each one richer and more profound than the last.

The weekend seemed to slip away like grains of sand through their fingers, leaving both Jack and Lucy with a bittersweet ache in their hearts. They had soaked up every precious moment together, their laughter echoing in the corners of the hotel room, and their quiet conversations wrapped in the warmth of familiarity. Yet, despite the time they spent entwined in each other's presence, it felt heartbreakingly insufficient.

As they stood at her door, the weight of their farewells loomed over them like an impending storm. The air was thick with unspoken words and longing glances, both aware that their lives were separated by vast distances—a cruel reminder of the reality they faced. Lucy's heart sank further at the thought of his departure. The world outside felt cold and uninviting, a stark contrast to the warmth they had shared.

Jack, sensing her sadness, took her hands in his, his grip assuring her that this was not goodbye, but merely a pause. "I'll be back next weekend," he promised, his voice a gentle balm to her worried soul. His words wrapped around her like a soft embrace, giving her a glimmer of hope amidst the heavy sorrow. Yet, the thought of him driving away made her chest tighten, and she wished desperately for time to freeze, allowing them a few more moments in their enchanting bubble.

With a tender kiss that lingered far too long, Jack finally pulled away, his eyes reflecting the same reluctance that she felt. Watching him walk down the path, each step felt like a countdown to disappointment. The sight of his car disappearing down the road hollowed her out, leaving her standing at the threshold, the crisp evening air biting at her skin.

Chapter Eleven

Once inside the familiar comfort of her home, Lucy sighed, the weight of solitude pressing down on her. Settling into her favourite chair, she cradled a warm mug in her hands and allowed herself to reminisce about their magical weekend—The sunset they watched painted in vibrant hues, the starlit sky they gazed upon, and their whispered secrets shared under the soft glow of the hotel room.

After a few moments, she picked up her phone, her heart fluttering with anticipation and a hint of sadness, and dialled Trisha's number. As the call connected, she knew it would be the perfect opportunity to relive every detail, each memory sparkling like a gem in her mind. Speaking to Trisha only fuelled Lucy's excitement for her blossoming romance, as Trisha's infectious joy echoed through the phone. The happiness in Lucy's voice was a stark contrast to the weariness that had coloured their past conversations, making Trisha feel as though she was chatting with a brand-new version of her friend. Trisha shared the thrilling news that she and Pablo had finally set a date for their wedding, a revelation that sent waves of elation coursing through Lucy.

As they talked late into the evening, the conversation flowed effortlessly from Trisha's upcoming wedding preparations to the tantalising notion of a similar future for Lucy and Jack. Each shared moment and dream built a vibrant construction of hope in Lucy's mind, binding together images of lace and laughter, vows exchanged under a canopy of blooming flowers.

When the call finally ended and the screen dimmed, Lucy found herself lost in a daydream, her heart fluttering at the thought of becoming Mrs. Lucy Archer. The thought was both exhilarating and bewildering. She had always dismissed the idea of marriage. Yet now, she could vividly picture a future where Jack would drop to one knee, a glimmer of hope and love in his eyes, and she wouldn't hesitate to say yes.

Puzzlement began to wash over her as she contemplated her emotions. After all, they had only met twice since working together, and their relationship was still in the preliminary stages, just a couple of months old. How could she feel so intensely about someone she barely knew? Was it irrational to dream of forever so soon, or had she finally, unexpectedly, fallen in love?

Time seemed to accelerate during the following week, almost as if it couldn't wait for Jack's return. When he finally appeared at her door, the sun dipped low, casting a hopeful glow over the evening. In his hands was a colourful bouquet of flowers, their colours radiant against the softening sky. The delicate fragrance of roses and lilies filled the air as he greeted her, planting kisses on her lips and showering her with affectionate words.

Lucy felt like she had encountered the embodiment of her dreams. Each night, as twilight descended while they were apart, Jack would call her, his voice wrapping around her like a warm blanket on a chilly evening. Their conversations flowed effortlessly, igniting within her a giddy elation that lingered long after they hung up.

She adored how Jack made her feel—his presence was like an intoxicating elixir, leaving her spellbound. She found herself yearning for him, as though his very essence completed her. Whenever he visited, he brought fresh flowers that he carefully selected, making their time together feel like a scene from a romantic film. On the days he couldn't come, he would surprise her with beautiful flower arrangements sent through the post, each delivery a testament to his affection.

Lucy had never known such tender devotion; it was as if she had been transformed into a princess, just as Jack often referred to her. One enchanting evening, beneath a canopy of shimmering stars, Jack took her hand, his eyes sparkling with sincerity. With a gentle yet confident demeanour, he asked her to be his girlfriend.

Without hesitation, she accepted, her heart fluttering like the wings of a butterfly set free. In that magical moment, Lucy realised that all of her hopes and dreams were materialising before her very eyes. Jack was nothing short of extraordinary, and now he was hers completely, intertwining their lives in a beautiful blanket of love and affection.

The next visit from Jack would cast a long shadow over the radiant romance they had nurtured. As the late afternoon sun filtered through the curtains, Jack sat across from Lucy, his expression a mixture of regret and resolve. He took a deep breath before breaking the heavy news that his trip to the Middle East had been unexpectedly moved up.

"I'll be gone for about a month," he said, his voice tinged with reluctance, "but if I can, I'll return sooner." His eyes, usually so bright, dimmed with the weight of the revelation. "The last thing I want is to leave you, but this has been planned long before I even met you, and I can't back out now."

As he spoke, Lucy's heart sank, the joyous moments they had shared flashing vividly in her mind—each laughter, each tender kiss, all now overshadowed by the looming uncertainty. Jack confided in her, his voice barely above a whisper, about the fear that gnawed at him—the idea of being in danger, of not making it back to her safe and sound.

Lucy felt a chill wash over her as she realised how real that fear could be. How could fate be so cruel? Just when she had found the man of her dreams, the universe threatened to snatch him away. They would only have one more precious visit before his departure, and she longed to make it unforgettable.

That night, as the stars twinkled like scattered diamonds across a velvet sky, Jack slept peacefully beside her, his soft breath rising and falling in a soothing rhythm. Lucy lay wide awake, her gaze tracing the contours of his face, memorising every detail—the gentle slope of his nose, the smooth contour of his shaven head, and most captivating of all, the depth of his striking grey-blue eyes.

"Why does he have to go away?" she thought, grappling with a fierce ache in her heart. In a moment of desperation, she considered what might happen if she simply didn't wake him up, if he missed his ferry. Would he be angry with her for holding him back?

Just as the thought settled heavily in her chest, he stirred. His eyes fluttered open, revealing those mesmerising shades of blue that seemed to dance with light and warmth. He smiled at her, and in that instant, the weight of her worries began to dissolve.

Lucy gazed deeply into his eyes, the world around them melting away as she felt a profound realisation wash over her—she was absolutely and irrevocably in love with this man, and the thought of losing him felt unbearable. In that fleeting moment, surrounded by the quiet intimacy of the night, she knew she would do anything to keep the spark of their love alive, no matter the distance that might lie ahead.

Jack's departure was steeped in emotion, the kind of bittersweet weight that lingered in the air like the morning fog. As he stood before Lucy, their hands intertwined, he shared the unsettling news that it would be several days before she'd hear from him again. The reality of his work loomed over them; the people he worked for would confiscate his phone before he boarded the ferry, a precaution shrouded in mystery and foreboding.

Lucy, her heart racing with a mix of concern and curiosity, pressed him for details about his trip to the Middle East. Yet, Jack remained oddly evasive, simply stating that his role involved working with offenders, a phrase that sent a shiver down her spine. He cautioned her, his voice low and serious, about the need to keep his two worlds separate; he couldn't allow the challenges of his life in the UK to blend with whatever awaited him overseas.

A wave of sadness washed over Lucy; her heart heavy with the fear of uncertainty. But interwoven with that sadness was a fragile thread of hope; Jack's carefulness suggested he was aware of the dangers he faced, and that awareness filled her with a longing for his safe return. Their embrace was a tender moment, warm and reassuring—a silent promise exchanged in the stillness. They shared a long, lingering kiss, one that seemed to encapsulate everything they felt for one another, as if trying to defy the distance that threatened to pull them apart.

As Jack drove away, disappearing into the soft glow of the morning light, Lucy felt a sense of emptiness envelop her. The door swung shut behind her, and a wave of emotion surged within her. She fought the tears that threatened to spill as she found herself drawn to her phone.

With trembling fingers, she began to type, her emotions flowing onto the screen: *"My darling Jack, I need you to know just how deeply I feel about you. I know I don't express it often, but I am completely, utterly in love with you. The thought of you leaving fills me with a dread that I may never see you again. I had to tell you before you don't have your phone anymore. I will miss you more than you can imagine; the very idea of living a moment without you is unbearable. Yet, here we are, cruelly separated by circumstances beyond our control. Please, my handsome man, be safe and return to me in one piece. You hold my heart, and I will love you always. — Lucy xxxx."*

A tear slipped down her cheek as she pressed send, the weight of her words hanging in the air long after the message vanished into the ether. Lucy received a message a couple of hours later, just before Jack's phone was taken from him. His words struck a chord deep within her: he expressed that he felt exactly the same way she did and promised that he would return to her safe. A wave of reassurance washed over Lucy as she read his message, but it was quickly overshadowed by a cloud of sadness, knowing it would be days before she could hear from him again, and even longer—weeks—before she would see him once more.

The next few days descended into a haze of misery for Lucy. Each passing hour intensified her longing to hear Jack's voice, the familiar comfort of his laughter and the warmth of his words. At work, the alteration in her demeanour didn't go unnoticed; her colleagues exchanged concerned glances and whispered among themselves. Though Lucy forced a smile and assured everyone that she was simply tired after restless nights, a gnawing ache settled in her chest. Jack had asked her to keep his trip a secret from their London office, insisting that it was crucial for both their sakes; the fear of jeopardising his job loomed large in his mind.

Despite her resolve to keep his secret, the weight of her solitude grew heavier. To combat her feelings, Lucy had confided only in her close friend, Mia. One evening, over steaming mugs of coffee, she revealed the truth about Jack's trip, her voice tinged with uncertainty as she admitted she wasn't entirely clear on what he was doing in the Middle East. Mia, with her curious eyes sparkling with intrigue, peppered Lucy with questions about the adventure, the danger, the unknown. Yet, Lucy found herself grappling with her own ignorance. Should she have pressed him for more details before he left? Would he have even opened up to her, or would he simply have continued to dance around her enquiries, evading her concerns with vague reassurances? The questions spiralled in her mind, leaving her feeling foolish for not digging deeper.

After a long, agonising four days that stretched endlessly in Lucy's mind, she finally received a much-anticipated email from Jack. Her heart raced as she opened it, her eyes scanning the words that danced across the screen. Jack's message was warm and reassuring, telling her that he was doing fine and that the job he was there to complete was progressing well. The relief washed over her, but what truly stirred her heart were his next words—how much he was missing her already. Lucy could almost hear his voice softly resonating in her head as he described how he found himself rushing through his tasks, longing to return to her sooner.

The mere thought of Jack coming back early sent a thrill through Lucy—an intoxicating mix of hope and excitement. She blinked in disbelief at the possibility, but his email left little room for doubt. She read and re-read those lines, each pass filling her with a sense of comfort and affection, as if she could feel his presence beside her.

Energised by the idea of him working diligently to return to her, Lucy's heart positively fluttered. It reaffirmed her feelings, solidifying her belief in the bond they shared. Inspired, she began to craft her reply, pouring out her heart onto the screen. She expressed her overwhelming happiness at hearing from him and confessed how truly miserable the days had been since he left. Lucy wrote about how each day blurred into the next, her life feeling achingly mundane and empty without him by her side.

She mentioned her work, a dull routine that offered little joy, but she also shared that she had spent some time with Mia. Lucy felt the need to explain that she had confided in Mia about Jack's trip, worried that it might make him angry. As she typed, she could almost sense Jack's reaction—his sincere understanding wrapped in gentle patience.

She concluded her email with a heartfelt declaration of her love for him and, in a burst of emotion, added around fifteen kisses at the end. Each kiss felt like a piece of her heart sent across the miles, carrying her longing and devotion directly to Jack. The next few days consisted of back-and-forth emails between the two, only one or two emails if Lucy was lucky as Jack explained he had needed to find internet cafés to email her from and these were few and far between. Lucy knew she couldn't receive messages from him throughout the day, but she felt so lucky every time she did receive an email from him. He was thinking about her everyday and that made her feel special.

One bright and crisp afternoon, as the sunlight filtered through the leaves, casting playful shadows on the ground, Lucy made her way through the busy streets to the garage. She was eagerly anticipating the moment she could get behind the wheel of her car, which had been in for its MOT, a routine that always left her a little on edge. Just as she neared the garage, her phone began to ring, the sound slicing through the peaceful afternoon air.

Seeing that it was an unknown number, her instinct was to ignore it; after all, unsolicited calls were a common nuisance. However, a nagging thought struck her—perhaps it was the garage, calling to update her on her car's status. With a deep breath, she answered.

As soon as she did, she was enveloped by the soft southern tones of her beautiful man, Jack. The familiarity of his voice sent a thrill down her spine, and she couldn't help but smile. How could it be? She felt a rush of warmth flood her heart as he explained how he had managed to borrow a phone from one of the security guards at the site where he was working. He had kept her number tucked safely in his pocket, determined to reach out the moment he had the chance.

Their conversation flowed effortlessly as they caught up, weaving their lives back together despite the distance separating them. They shared laughter and soft whispers of their love, relishing the connection that was as strong as ever. Jack's words brought waves of joy as he revealed that, despite only being apart for a couple of weeks, there was a chance he could return home in just a few days. Lucy felt her heart soar; the excitement bubbled within her like a fizzy drink ready to overflow.

However, as the call came to an end, silence settled back over her. The day stretched ahead, feeling both full of promise and heavy with uncertainty. The next day, Jack sent her a daily email, his words painting a cautious picture of his journey south. He mentioned the possibility of danger lurking ahead, and Lucy felt a knot tighten in her stomach. Instinctively, she worried for his safety but pushed the anxiety aside, knowing he was doing everything he could to return to her.

The following day, she met her mother and brother for lunch—a rare occasion that brought her comfort and joy. They shared laughter, exchanged stories, and indulged in delicious food, allowing the worries about Jack to fade into the background, if only temporarily. However, as the evening drew near, unease crept back in, manifesting into a gnawing feeling deep within her. It had now been a whole twenty-four hours since she had last heard from Jack, and an unsettling feeling clutched at her heart—a premonition that something might be wrong. She made the decision to pour her heart into a letter for Jack, the man who had become her anchor in a tumultuous sea of uncertainty. With trembling hands, she crafted sentences that spilled forth her deepest fears—that the worst had indeed happened, and the gnawing ache of potential loss was suffocating. In flowing ink, she expressed how empty her existence would feel without him. Lucy imagined handing it to him when he finally returned, a tangible piece of her heart to lay bare before him.

That night, as she surrendered to sleep, vivid memories danced through her mind like fireflies in the dark. She relived the warmth of their last embrace, the soft whispers of affection that lingered in the air, and the way their bodies had entwined, creating a fleeting sense of oneness that felt almost sacred. When morning light broke, it was met with an urgent longing—a desperate hope for an email from Jack. She found herself checking her inbox obsessively throughout the day, even resorting to calling in sick to work, a decision that felt outrageous yet necessary.

As twilight descended, Lucy returned home, the car's interior filled with the soothing melodies that usually brought her solace. Her phone rested in its cradle, silent, yet her mind raced with anxiety. Reassurance had initially washed over her when Jack had assured her, she was his next of kin, the knowledge that she would be informed of any dire news offering a semblance of comfort. But as the days dragged on and silence stretched between them, doubt crept in.

Then, without warning, her phone buzzed, vibrating against the smooth surface of the console. Her heart leapt into her throat as a notification flashed before her eyes—an email from Jack. She abruptly pulled over. With a racing heart, she opened the email, each word threatening to plunge her deeper into despair. The moment felt suspended in time, the world around her fading away as she immersed herself in the message that could alter everything.

Chapter Twelve

The email confirmed her worst fears. Jack explained that he was in the hospital after being involved in an explosion at one of the houses he was visiting. He shared that everyone else in the house hadn't made it out alive, and he had been pulled from the wreckage by some local people who witnessed the commotion. Jack described suffering a seizure, which the paramedics had difficulty controlling, and he was rushed north to a major hospital to treat his injuries. He mentioned that he was covered in burns and had broken several bones, but somehow, he had managed to survive. In his email, he conveyed that he had focused on his promise to return to her safely.

Lucy sat in her car, completely distraught, her heart pounding in her chest as waves of anxiety washed over her. Her hands trembled slightly as she read the cryptic email for the third time, a sinking feeling in her stomach that only deepened with each passing moment. All she wanted was to catch the next flight, to be with him, but an overwhelming sense of helplessness gripped her—she didn't even know where he was.

"Why hadn't anyone told me what had happened?" she whisper-shouted into the silence of her dimly lit car, her voice cracking under the weight of her fears. As his next of kin, she felt it was her right, her duty, to be informed, to understand the gravity of the situation.

With a heavy heart, she composed her reply, the words spilling out in a rush of disbelief and anguish. Her mind raced, filled with dark imaginings of what she believed had occurred. Deep down, she felt an unsettling certainty; something terrible had happened.

Jack had always insisted that their bond was special—that they shared a connection that transcended the ordinary. They could sense each other's emotions, feel each other's joys and sorrows as if they were intertwined. As she hit send, tears slipped down her cheeks, each one a testament to her unwavering love and the dread that echoed in her mind. She had just known something was wrong. Though a chill of dread coursed through Lucy at the thought of anything else occurring to Jack, a flicker of reassurance warmed her heart, knowing they had reestablished communication. The uncertainty of his well-being had been weighing heavily on her, and the thought of him alone only deepened her anxiety. Regular updates were crucial; she needed the comfort of his words to quell her fears.

Fortunately, Jack was often able to commandeer the old computer stationed in the bustling nurses' station, a hub of constant chatter and activity. There, under the fluorescent lights that hummed overhead, he would tap out email after email, each one a lifeline to Lucy. She cherished every message, each one a small window into his world, a reassurance that he was still fighting and that he was okay.

Jack had also crafted a plan to seize the phone from the gruff man in the adjacent bay whenever he found a moment. With determination shining in his eyes, he promised Lucy, he would call her as soon as he could, a promise that filled her with hope amidst the lingering shadows of fear. The thought of hearing his voice again—full of life and spirit—was something she clung to, brightening the corners of her worried mind. For a few days, their communication unfolded through the cool glow of email, a lifeline tethering Lucy to Jack as he lay in the sterile confines of his hospital room. Each message exchanged was laced with an undercurrent of worry; Lucy could sense the shadows creeping deeper into Jack's mind, pulling him further into the void of his depression. His longing to leave the hospital was palpable, an ache that resonated with her own desire to have him home, where they could rebuild the fragments of their life together.

Yet, in her heart, Lucy knew that the hospital was where Jack truly needed to be. The thought of him navigating the world outside—vulnerable and raw, still grappling with the weight of his injuries—

filled her with dread. With a heavy heart, she found herself crafting her words carefully, encouraging him to remain under the watchful eyes of the medical staff who could provide the care he desperately required. Jack, in the end, acquiesced, though it was clear from his responses that his consent came tinged with reluctance and frustration. The battle between his longing for freedom and the necessity of healing played out in every line of their correspondence, leaving Lucy feeling both grateful and heartbroken. He assured Lucy in a steady voice, filled with a warmth that travelled through the phone line, that he was on the mend, his humour rekindling like a flame long thought extinguished. He promised her he would be home in time for her birthday, just as he had vowed before the accident. "It would be wonderful if you could make it home," she said softly, her heart aching with hope. "But it's okay if you can't. Your health is what matters most."

As if sensing the weight of her anxiety, their conversation swiftly shifted back to the familiar cadence they cherished. Jack launched into animated tales about his escapades in the hospital, painting pictures of laughter amidst the chaos. He recounted his antics with playful exaggeration, detailing the mischievous pranks he had played on the staff—like stealing the nurse's pen and pretending it had vanished into thin air. "She doesn't like me," he chuckled, and Lucy couldn't help but laugh along, the sound bubbling like a spring. Her laughter, bright and melodious, momentarily chased away the shadows of worry that had crept in. In those moments, it was easy to forget the gravity of the situation, lost in the warmth of their shared connection.

After a couple of restless days of sending emails into the silence, Lucy found herself returning home from work, her heart heavy with unease. The familiar rhythm of Jack's daily messages had abruptly ceased, leaving a void in her evening routine. She paced around her small living room, the ticking of the clock echoing her growing anxiety. What could have possibly happened to him? Was he okay?

Later that evening, as she settled onto the couch with a cup of coffee, her phone lit up with a message from an unfamiliar number. With a mix of hope and trepidation, she opened it, her breath catching in her throat. It was Jack. He had managed to leave the hospital and, against all odds, found a ride across the border. Her heart raced as she read his words: he was trying to find his way home to her.

He had sent the message using the phone of a sympathetic stranger who had given him a lift, emphasising that once he secured a phone of his own, he would reach out again. His thoughtfulness in sending this message made her chest swell with affection, but the worry still lingered.

Days passed, and the silence returned, thick and unyielding. Lucy's anxiety intensified until finally, an email arrived—this time from someone named Jacob. As she read through the message, confusion morphed into concern. Jacob introduced himself as Jack's boss. He painted a troubling picture, explaining that Jack was stubbornly refusing to follow medical advice, insisting instead on returning home to her.

Jacob's words were laced with urgency as he explained that Jack needed immediate care at a hospital in France—the very place he had reached but was unwilling to stay. The request was clear: Lucy needed to send a message affirming her desire for Jack to get the help he required, rather than rush home for her birthday. Jacob assured her that if she complied, he would ensure Jack received a phone so they could speak, providing a glimmer of hope amid her worry.

Lucy felt torn between her desire for Jack to be by her side on her birthday and her deep-rooted need for him to be healthy. She took a deep breath, hoping desperately that her love would guide them both through this tumultuous time.

Lucy felt a heavy weight in her chest as the days dragged on without a word from either Jacob or Jack. The bright sun shining through her window on the morning of her birthday did little to lift her spirits; instead, it only served as a stark contrast to the deep-rooted sadness consuming her. Today, of all days, she longed for the warmth of Jack's presence beside her, the man who had filled her thoughts and dreams with hope and love.

As she sat on the edge of her bed, the scent of her favourite lavender candles burning in the air, she couldn't shake the unsettling feeling gnawing at her. Her phone rang, pulling her from her reverie. It was Dale, and as they spoke, his voice offered a semblance of comfort.

He assured her that Jack would be fine, but those words felt like an incomplete puzzle piece. Lucy had confided in Dale about Jack's departure, sharing only fragments of the story since details were scarce, leaving her grasping at straws whenever she tried to make sense of it all.

As the hours slipped by, Lucy made a conscious decision to change her mindset. She could either wallow in despair or embrace the possibility of a bright future that lay ahead—the future she and Jack had begun to build. With a deep breath, she resolved to shake off the melancholy that threatened to consume her. She wouldn't let this birthday define her; after all, Jack's absence didn't mean he didn't care.

With those thoughts, Lucy began to envision their dreams together traveling to unfamiliar places, sharing laughter over candlelit dinners, and building a life filled with love. She let her imagination drift away, allowing it to paint vibrant scenes of what could be. Lucy's birthday ended like a fleeting shadow, almost as quickly as it had come. As she lay on her bed, she mindlessly scrolled through her social media feed, heart warmed by the flurry of kind birthday messages that lit up her notifications. Each heartfelt wish and cute meme brought a smile to her face, but a lingering disappointment tugged at her heart as she realised there was no special greeting from Jack—his absence felt like a dull ache.

Later that evening, wrapped snugly in her favourite blanket with a novel in her lap, Lucy tried to lose herself in the world of fiction. However, the words on the pages blurred into a backdrop as her mind drifted away, weaving its own narrative. She closed her eyes and let her thoughts swirl around the enigmatic figure of Jack. He had always been a puzzle wrapped in an alluring mystery, and now, with his recent trip still shrouded in secrecy, her curiosity overflowed.

She couldn't shake the feeling that there was so much more to Jack than he let on. The way he spoke about his "other employer" sent shivers of intrigue down her spine. Who were these people he worked for? What secrets did they hold? Each question hung in the air, begging for answers and filling her with an insatiable desire to uncover his truth. Lucy's heart raced at the thought of investigating further, feeling like a detective in her own unfolding story. She was determined to peel back the layers of Jack's life and discover the man hiding beneath the surface, one captivating clue at a time.

A soft glimmer of sunlight peeked through the curtains, gently rousing Lucy from a restless sleep. Ever since Jack had departed, her nights had transformed into a labyrinth of worry and longing, each thought about him swirling chaotically in her mind. Last night had been particularly gruelling, filled with vivid dreams that left her more exhausted than before.

Fuelled by a need for distraction, she turned up her favourite playlist, allowing the vibrant tunes to fill the air like a warm embrace. The rhythm pulsed through her veins, igniting a spark of energy within her. Lucy danced around the living room, her voice soaring alongside the music as she tackled the neglected corners of her home, each note lifting her spirits higher.

Just as a particularly catchy chorus swept her up in joy, her phone lighting up with a call abruptly interrupted the moment. The screen glowed with Jack's name, bold and bright, as if it were a beacon cutting through the fog of her unease. Eagerly, Lucy rushed to answer, her heart racing at the thought of him returning to her.

"Oh my god, hi!" she squealed into the phone, her voice filled with uncontainable excitement.

"Hi!" he replied, his smooth southern drawl wrapping around her like a comforting blanket. "How are you?"

Lucy could barely contain her glee. "I'm so much better seeing you ringing me!" she exclaimed, her heart swelling at the sound of his voice. "I've been so looking forward to hearing from you!"

Jack continued, his words weaving in and out as he explained that he was on his way to her, but an unexpected complication had forced him to abandon his plans to drive. "I'll explain everything when I get there," he promised, and Lucy's heart raced with anticipation.

They chatted about the details of his trip, the ups and downs of his health, their voices mingling in a melody of familiarity. With every exchanged word, the distance between them seemed to shrink. They decided to delve deeper into their conversation when she would pick him up from the train station, and Lucy couldn't help but grin, feeling the warmth of hope envelop her as she anticipated their reunion.

That evening, as twilight cloaked the town in shades of deep indigo and gold, Jack finally contacted Lucy to let her know he was nearing the train station where they had last exchanged longing glances. With a heart full of anticipation, she hopped into her car, the engine purring to life beneath her eager hands. She raced through the streets, her pulse quickening with every turn as she envisioned their reunion.

Upon arriving, she parked with a sense of urgency and dashed towards the station, her breaths coming in excited huffs. As she started to ascend the ramp to the station entrance, her eyes caught sight of him—her beautiful man. Jack approached, a rucksack slung over his shoulder, dressed in grey jeans that hugged his frame and a matching bubble jacket that seemed to echo the warmth she felt inside. Yet, he looked a bit dishevelled, his stubble hinting it had been far too long since he had last shaved. This raw, unrefined version of Jack was a stark contrast to the polished man she had known, but even in this rugged state, he was utterly irresistible to her.

As soon as Lucy's gaze locked onto Jack's, pure glee bubbled forth, erupting in a loud cry of excitement that sliced through the cool evening air. She sprinted toward him, her feet pounding against the pavement, and Jack mirrored her energy, quickening his pace until they were wrapped in each other's arms, creating a cocoon of warmth amidst the night's chill. The world around them faded as they held one another tightly, their hearts beating in sync beneath the soft glow of the streetlights that illuminated their joyous reunion.

Over the next few days, they found solace in each other's presence. They nestled together, words flowing like a gentle stream as they shared stories, sadness and laughter, recounting every detail of the time apart. The scent of Jack, mingling with hints of the outdoors and adventure, filled Lucy's senses, making her feel both comforted and alive.

Each morning, she meticulously tended to the various wounds on Jack's body, marks of his journey that told silent tales of struggle and survival. As she carefully cleaned and bandaged each scar, her fingertips danced along his skin, tracing the lines that felt like roadmaps of their experiences yet to be shared. She felt drawn to these stories, each scar whispering of trials faced and battles fought. Lucy knew Jack would eventually open up about his past, but for now, she cherished the simple joy of being in his protective embrace.

The worry that had gnawed at her heart during his absence began to dissipate like morning mist under the sun. Their reunion was everything Lucy had dreamed it would be—filled with warmth, connection, and the promise of love rekindled. In Jack's arms, she felt an overwhelming sense of safety, a cocoon where nothing else mattered.

Lucy and Jack spent every waking moment together over the next few days, their laughter intertwining with the quiet hum of life around them. The sun-drenched mornings turned to starlit nights, with their conversations ebbing and flowing like the tide. It was during one of these tranquil moments, wrapped in the warmth of their shared connection, that Jack revealed he would soon have to leave for a meeting in London with his "other employer." The weight of that news hung heavy in the air.

Days passed, and Lucy finally found the courage to ask what had led to Jack's sudden absence before. Jack sighed deeply, a shadow crossing his face. "There's a lot to explain," he said, his voice edged with a mix of apprehension and resolve. As Jack began to unveil his story, his words painted a picture of a life she had never imagined. He spoke of his work as an intelligence officer, diving into the murky depths of a world fraught with danger. With each revelation, Lucy's pulse quickened. Jack had been sourcing vital information from individuals scattered across the Middle East; they were caught in a web of turmoil and peril.

He hesitated for a moment before confiding that among those he worked with were offenders, dangerous men with secrets lurking in their shadows. His mission was to keep a watchful eye on them— unbeknownst to Lucy, he had been wading through treacherous waters, all to protect her. The gravity of his words struck Lucy like a bolt of lightning; her mind struggled to grasp the enormity of what he was sharing.

"I didn't want to burden you with this," Jack confessed, running a hand over his head, a gesture that betrayed his inner turmoil. "I thought it would keep you safe." Lucy's heart raced as she processed his confession, grappling with the image of the man she had fallen for—a man shrouded in secrecy, living a life fraught with danger.

Questions swirled in her mind like autumn leaves caught in a whirlwind. Who was this man sitting next to her? How had he woven himself into the fabric of her life, leaving an imprint on her heart? She had grown to love him, yet she felt as if she barely knew him. The room seemed to shrink around them, filled with unspoken fears and uncertainties.

Jack continued, his voice lower now, as if fearing to disturb the weight of his revelations. "There's so much more to this, Lucy, but I can't tell you everything. I would be putting myself in serious danger." His eyes locked onto hers, a mixture of sincerity and sorrow reflected in their depths. In that moment, Lucy realised that the man she had fallen for was both a stranger and someone she felt deeply connected to, a juxtaposition that left her dizzy with emotion. She leaned back, overwhelmed, aware that the love she felt was tangled in a web of secrets that could shake their world to its core. Jack informed Lucy that he had to leave for London for a few days to discuss the recent events that had unfolded in the Middle East. The thought of his absence struck a chord deep within her; Lucy had already spent what felt like an eternity apart from Jack, and the idea of wasting even more precious time made her stomach churn with anxiety. She yearned for his presence, yet he was resolute, insisting he needed to leave again.

As she drove him to the station, a cloud of uncertainty began to swirl in her mind. Why was he going back so soon? Was there something more going on beneath the surface that he wasn't revealing? Just days ago, Jack had been so eager to return to her, and now, here he was, about to board a train that would take him away once more. With each mile that passed, her heart sank further.

When they arrived, the atmosphere felt sombre, as if time itself was conspiring against them. Lucy parked the car in the fading light of the evening, an eerie stillness settling over her. Jack's hands, usually so confident and strong, now fidgeted nervously as he gathered his things, a hint of conflict flickering across his face. She wanted to reach out, to pull him back and tell him to stay, but she knew he needed to fulfil this obligation.

As they shared a long, tearful goodbye, their emotions intertwined like a tangible force in the cool air. Lucy felt the weight of her disappointment almost suffocating, but she masked it behind a veneer of strength. Jack made a promise, his voice steady and sincere, vowing that this wouldn't be the start of a recurring separation. He assured her that once the storm passed, he would be back in his "normal" job in London, visiting her regularly. The thought of building their lives together, possibly moving in, painted a future she longed for.

With one last, lingering hug that felt as if it could bridge the distance between them, Lucy released him, watching as he turned to walk toward the train platform. The world around her seemed to blur as her heart ached with solitude. She turned to get back into the car, a lump swelling in her throat.

Just as she settled into the driver's seat, her phone buzzed, pulling her from her thoughts. It was a message from Jack, lighting up the dark space around her. His words spilled out, filling the void he had left behind. He wrote of her beauty, both inside and out, intoxicating her with sweet declarations of love and admiration. He expressed his eagerness to spend the rest of his life with her, a thread of hope weaving through the melancholy. And in that moment, despite the heavy cloud of longing and uncertainty, Lucy felt a flicker of warmth amidst the sorrow, a promise that this separation would be the last.

While away, Jack had become increasingly distant, leaving Lucy to grapple with a whirlwind of emotions. Initially, he showered her with attention, ringing her frequently, engaging in heartfelt video calls, and filling her phone with messages that lit up her screen like fireworks. In those moments, Lucy felt like the luckiest woman alive, enchanted by her mystery man, even though she sensed he carried a hidden darker side. She knew that at some point, she would need to dig deeper, to unravel the enigma that was Jack, but she convinced herself that those questions could wait until they were back on solid ground.

However, after that initial flurry of affection, a heavy silence settled in. Days turned into an agonising stretch of no messages, no calls—Jack wasn't even reading her texts. Lucy felt an overwhelming sense of loneliness, an emptiness that clung to her like a thick fog. Why had he vanished on her? A wave of anxiety crashed over her, and a troubling thought began to form: what if he wasn't, okay? What if he was reaching out for her in his own way, needing her support, but she was too far away to lend a hand?

Deciding she couldn't stay idle any longer, Lucy shared her concerns with her friend Adrian, a steadfast companion from work. Together, they hatched a plan: they would drive to London and find Jack. The mere thought of the road trip infused Lucy with a sense of purpose, a glimmer of hope amidst her worry.

As they sat together planning their journey, the warm glow of camaraderie enveloped them. They decided to take Lucy's car, a reliable little hatchback that had seen them through many adventures. They would take turns behind the wheel, driving through the picturesque English countryside, sharing the road just as they shared their excitement for the trip.

Adrian was a lovely man—his kind eyes and easy smile put Lucy at ease. He was a few years younger, yet exuded a wisdom beyond his years, well-rooted in a stable relationship with his partner, Lee. Despite their time apart since leaving Dale House, the bond between Lucy and Adrian felt as strong as ever, as if no time had passed. The excitement of the road trip mingled with the underlying worry for Jack, but in that moment, they were united in their quest, ready to face whatever awaited them in London.

While Lucy and Adrian sat together, their laughter mingling with the warm afternoon air, they delved into exciting plans for their upcoming adventure to London. The sun cast a golden glow around them as Lucy glanced at her phone, noticing that Jack had finally read her messages but had remained frustratingly silent. A flutter of anxiety twisted in her stomach, prompting her to ask Adrian what he thought it meant.

Adrian, leaning back against the bench, furrowed his brow and replied, "I'm not sure, Lucy. He might just be busy." Just as her unease began to settle, a notification chimed on her phone, and she opened a voice message from Jack.

"Hey, Lucy… I'm fine. No need to come to London; I'm heading back to yours tonight."

A wave of disbelief washed over her, quickly followed by an intoxicating rush of warmth and excitement. Jack was coming back to be with her. The thought filled her with a giddy joy, and she could already picture the moment they'd be reunited, the way he would wrap her in his arms, making her feel safe and cherished.

After saying their goodbyes, Lucy parted ways with Adrian and hurried home, her mind racing with preparations for Jack's return. The motorway stretched ahead, and she drove with determination, the wind whipping through the open windows as she anticipated the reunion. Once home, she threw herself into a flurry of activity, tidying up her cosy living space, fluffing cushions, and making sure everything looked perfect.

With her house sparkling and herself freshly showered and dressed, Lucy settled into a chair, glancing occasionally at her phone, the weight of anticipation heavy in the air. Hours passed, and a creeping sense of uncertainty began to gnaw at her. What time would Jack arrive? He hadn't provided a clear timeframe, but her heart raced in hope that he would appear soon.

Finally, a message from Jack broke the silence: "I'm almost back." A bolt of energy surged through her. Without a moment's hesitation, Lucy dashed outside, not even bothering to grab her jacket, the cool evening air brushing against her skin. She jumped in her car and sped down the road, her heart beating faster with every passing moment.

However, as she approached, she realised she might not be ready for the man who would soon walk through her door. The excitement mingled with a twinge of anxiety, making her pulse race as she pulled into the carpark, eager and anxious for their reunion.

Lucy sat anxiously in her car outside the bustling coach station, the chilly evening air wrapping around her like a tight cloak. Her heart raced with uncertainty as she waited for Jack to join her. The echoes of their recent silence loomed large in her mind, stirring feelings of unease. She couldn't shake the nagging thought that Jack's return was coerced, a result of some unseen pressure rather than a genuine desire to reconnect. Fear coiled in her chest like a heavy weight, causing an ache that made it hard to breathe.

Just then, she spotted him—tall and handsome, the very image of the man she had fallen for during their time together at work. He approached her car with an easy confidence, the soft glow of the setting sun illuminating his sharp features. To her surprise, he carried a vibrant bouquet of flowers, their colours standing out against the ashen backdrop of the station. Jack's face lit up with a radiant smile as he opened the back door, placing his bag inside with a practiced ease before sliding into the front passenger seat.

In that moment, he leaned towards her, capturing her in a fervent kiss that sent a jolt of warmth through her. The world outside faded away, and for a fleeting instant, it felt as though nothing else mattered. He pulled back, his eyes sparkling with affection as he handed her the flowers, softly proclaiming, "There's my beautiful girl!" A wave of relief washed over Lucy, the tension in her body easing as she realised, he wasn't there to hurt her.

As they drove away, the rhythmic hum of the engine provided a comforting backdrop to their conversation. Lucy shared her feelings of dread during their days apart, her voice trembling slightly with vulnerability as she recounted how deeply she had worried about him. Jack listened intently, his expression turning serious as he apologised. He explained how he had struggled with certain details while coordinating his recent trip to the Middle East.

Though Lucy sensed the undercurrent of despair that coloured his words, she decided to set aside her concerns for the moment. Instead, she chose to bask in the warmth of their reunion, eager to cherish every second they had together. Tonight was about reconnecting and savouring the joy of having Jack back in her life—she intended to make the most of it and hold onto the happiness that was finally within reach.

Upon returning to the sanctuary of her home, Lucy quickly wrapped herself in a soft, inviting blanket, its warmth enveloping her like a reassuring embrace. She and Jack nestled together on the plush sofa, the flickering glow of the television casting a serene light across the room. Although they sat close, Jack was unusually quiet, his words scarce and weighed down by an air of contemplation. Lucy glanced sideways; her heart heavy with concern as she wondered what burden he carried. Deep down, she trusted that when Jack was ready to share his thoughts, he would, and she felt a sense of calmness in their silent connection.

As the night unfolded, they sank deeper under the comfort of their fleece blanket, the world outside fading away into the distance. The gentle rhythm of the TV droned on, but they didn't need conversation to connect. They merely held each other, their bodies fitting together perfectly, like pieces of a long-lost puzzle. In that tender moment, Lucy felt an overwhelming sense of peace wash over her, as if time itself had come to a halt. The comfort of Jack's presence filled the room with unspoken promises, and she could have easily spent eternity lost in that tranquil embrace.

The following day brought with it the heaviness of reality. Jack opened up to Lucy about his harrowing experience in London, his voice thick with emotion. He recounted the tragic events surrounding the attack on the house he had been visiting in the middle east, his usually bright eyes clouded with pain and disbelief. It shook Lucy to her core. How could anyone possibly blame Jack for the tragic loss of life? He had been a victim too, injured and scarred, carrying wounds that would linger longer than any physical injury. The thought ignited a fierce protectiveness within her; he was a hero in her eyes, brave for what he faced and even braver for sharing it with her.

Jack filled the next week with more memories and struggles as he stayed with Lucy, but all too soon, the inevitable day arrived when he had to return to work. Lucy's heart sank at the thought of him leaving. She understood the necessity of his job, yet the heaviness in her chest spoke of her reluctance to part. However, Jack lightened her spirits when he promised he'd return the following weekend. His reassuring words painted a picture of hope, and Lucy found solace in knowing that even a brief separation would ultimately lead to their joyous reunion. Each day became a wish cast toward the weekend—a countdown filled with anticipation, where she could once again find comfort in Jack's arms.

For the next few weeks, Lucy and Jack eagerly met up every weekend, their time together filled with laughter and meaningful conversations that deepened their connection. Each encounter felt like peeling away the layers of an onion, revealing more about their lives and personalities. Under the gentle glow of streetlights or the cosy ambiance of a luxurious hotel room, Jack shared stories that made Lucy's heart race—stories of a tumultuous past that felt almost surreal.

With a heavy sigh, Jack recounted his chequered history, his voice tinged with a mix of regret and vulnerability. He spoke of his younger years spent in the shadows, where he had tangled himself in a life of crime. The words spilled from his lips like a dark cloud, painting a picture of a man once associated with drugs and weapons—each tale more chilling than the last. Lucy listened, wide-eyed and captivated, struggling to reconcile the loving, attentive man before her with the hardened figure he described. The very thought of him as someone who had harmed others, even for money, felt like a dagger to her heart.

How could this kind, tender soul, who treated her with such care and adoration, ever inflict pain? Her mind raced, replaying the moments when Jack had held her close, his eyes soft with affection. She couldn't fathom that the man she believed to be her perfect match could harbour a past so filled with darkness. It was impossible to imagine him as anything but her protector, someone who would only act in defence of her if danger ever approached.

Lucy sat on the edge of her sofa, the early morning light filtering through the curtain, casting soft shadows across the room. Her thoughts lingered on the haunting words Jack had left her with before heading off to work again. She clenched the fabric of her blanket, the fabric cool against her skin, as memories of his chilling tales swirled in her mind. Jack had shared horrifying stories of his past—tales filled with regret and darkness that would make anyone shudder. But despite that, her heart remained stubbornly tethered to him.

What was it about Jack that ensnared her so completely? It was as if an invisible thread bound her to him, one that she couldn't quite understand, much less break. The man before her was a contrast to the ghosts of his past, and yet she couldn't ignore the fierce longing she felt for a future with him. Lucy often caught herself daydreaming of what their life could be: shared laughter, lazy Sunday mornings, and quiet evenings filled with whispered conversations. The idea of a life entwined with Jack was intoxicating, even if it remained shrouded in shadows.

Puzzling over her feelings felt almost like a betrayal, as she knew the horrors he had revealed. But love, with all its complexities, seemed to transcend reason. She shook her head, trying to dismiss the erratic sense of devotion that surged within her. She wouldn't speak of his past to anyone else—this was their secret, one that felt too heavy to share. In her heart, she held onto the belief that Jack had transformed into someone new. He was not the monster his past had conjured; rather, he was the man who had captured her heart, and she was determined to see him that way.

Chapter Thirteen

Lucy found it hard to fear Jack; after all, he was her protector, the love of her life. How could she harbour any fear for the man who had wrapped her in the warmth of his embrace, whose laughter danced through her soul like sunlight streaming through tree branches? Jack's presence was intoxicating, yet beneath that charming exterior lay a shadowy side that sometimes sent chills up her spine. The unsettling stories he shared about his past life left her with a lingering worry— could he still be entangled in that dangerous world?

He had openly admitted to her that remnants of his former life still lingered, whispers of old acquaintances who operated in the shadows. Yet, he had also made a solemn promise: he was no longer a part of that life, and he would never again inflict harm on others for money. With each word, Lucy found herself comforted by his declarations, clinging to the belief that his grim tales were nothing but fabrications of a wild imagination seeking to make sense of darkness. She resolved to banish the unease from her heart, determined to erase the memories of his past as if they were ghosts fading into the mist.

As the weekend arrived and Jack returned, an anticipated thrill surged within Lucy. They made elaborate plans for a summer party, a vibrant celebration of life, love, and laughter. The thought of slipping into matching outfits made her heart flutter with giddy excitement; she could already envision their first dance under the stars, swaying together, lost in a melody that echoed their shared dreams. She felt as though she was enveloped in a shimmering, indestructible bubble, a sanctuary where nothing could disturb her bliss.

Every moment of anticipation felt overwhelming, filling her with a joy that radiated from her very core. Everything had finally returned to its rightful place, and Lucy was wholly and utterly in love, savouring the sweetness of a happiness she believed no one could ever take away from her.

As the weekend slipped into its final hours, casting a warm golden haze over the room, Jack began the bittersweet ritual of packing up his belongings. The soft rustle of fabric and the muffled thud of items being stowed created a sense of dread in the pit of his stomach. Just as he zipped up his duffel bag, his phone vibrated insistently on the table, breaking the serene silence. The weight of the conversation that was about to unfold settled heavily on him.

Moments later, Jack found himself in front of Lucy, whose expression shifted from curiosity to shock as he revealed the news. "I have to go away again for my 'other employer,'" he said, the words falling from his lips like stones. Lucy's heart sank. The promise he had made just a couple of months before echoed cruelly in her mind: he would not leave again. They had begun to weave the fabric of a new life together, filled with hopes of living together, shared mornings, and plans for a future that seemed within reach. Instead, the illusion shattered, leaving only shards of disappointment.

Lucy felt deflated, as if a deflating balloon lost its vibrancy and floated aimlessly to the ground. Would this cycle of farewell ever end? Or was she destined to play the part of the anxious girlfriend, forever waiting for him to return from distant lands, haunted by the spectres of danger that lurked in the shadows of his secretive profession?

In the quiet solitude of her thoughts, she recalled the strange incidents that had started to unfurl in his absence. Jack would often leave her home, claiming he was just popping out for milk or a stroll to clear his head. Each time he returned, however, he would bear unexpected injuries — a bruise decorating his forearm, a bandage wrapped around his hand. His tales of accidents, falling over a curb or tripping on a misplaced stone, would initially soothe her racing heart. But beneath the surface, a nagging instinct whispered that something was amiss.

Deep down, Lucy couldn't shake the feeling that the man she loved was shrouded in a web of secrets, and the truth lingered just out of reach, waiting to unravel.

Jack departed for London, leaving Lucy in a swirl of anxious thoughts. The moment he walked out the door, an unsettling knot formed in her stomach, a familiar feeling from the last time he had set off on a trip. Anxiety gnawed at her as she recalled how close she had come to losing him during that journey. Now, the fear intensified with the knowledge that he was heading for Syria, a place fraught with dangers that seemed all too real.

As the evening shadows lengthened around her, Lucy couldn't shake off the heaviness in her heart. She wandered through her home, tracing her fingers over the edges of framed photographs, each one a snapshot of happier times—a time when laughter filled the air, and their future felt brimming with promise. But now, those moments felt distant and fragile, as if a single gust of wind could scatter them.

She sank onto the couch, staring at the empty space where Jack usually sat. In the stillness, her mind raced with thoughts of the life she yearned for—a life filled with peace and safety, the kind she had always envisioned sharing with him. Yet, as much as she longed for that tranquillity, she grappled with the harsh reality of his profession and the risks that came with it.

With each tick of the clock, the weight of uncertainty pressed down on her. Could she truly build the life she dreamt of with a man who faced such perilous adventures? But then, an undeniable truth surfaced through the haze of her fears—Jack was the only one for her. No matter how many times she questioned their future or how often his choices led her to the brink of despair, her heart remained steadfast.

Lucy exhaled slowly, realising that her love for him was unwavering, unwavering against the tide of fear and doubt. As the night deepened, she found a flicker of resolve within her; she would stand by his side, no matter the storms that lay ahead. For in her heart, she knew that Jack was worth every sleepless night and every moment of uncertainty.

Although Lucy felt a knot of anxiety tightening in her stomach at the thought of Jack's upcoming trip, a swell of pride surged within her as well. She envisioned him out there, braving the unknown and risking his own safety in a courageous quest to rescue someone from the clutches of almost certain peril. The image of her handsome man, steadfast and fearless, filled her heart with admiration. Yet, beneath that pride, her thoughts danced nervously around the possibility that the trip might disrupt their carefully laid plans for the party.

When Lucy and Jack spoke on the phone, the warmth of his familiar voice washed over her, momentarily easing her worries. He confirmed the dates of his trip, his tone steady and reassuring, as he vowed to her that he would do everything in his power to return in time for the celebration. She felt a wave of relief flood through her; she trusted Jack's word implicitly, confident that he would keep his promise. In her heart, she knew that the only commitments he had ever struggled to uphold were those concerning his health—a reality she had come to accept, no matter how much it weighed on her.

Despite the gnawing unease she tried to banish from her mind, Lucy couldn't shake the thought of him not returning from this mission. However, a fierce conviction settled in her heart: she believed in his strength and relentless spirit. Jack was a force to be reckoned with, and she had no doubt that he would fight tooth and nail to come back to her, not just for himself, but for the love they shared. With that thought nestled firmly in her mind, she pushed aside her fears, clinging to the hope that their future moments together were just around the corner.

As the days dwindled down to his departure, Lucy was consumed by an overwhelming sense of dread. Each moment echoed the impending separation, deepening the hollow ache in her chest. Jack and Lucy had grown inseparable, their bond blossoming into a profound intimacy that both thrilled and bewildered her. They found joy in the simplest moments together—sharing laughter over breakfast, stealing kisses under the starry skies, and getting lost in conversations that stretched long into the night. Yet, every time Jack prepared to leave for work, their joyful moments gave way to heated arguments fuelled by the fear of losing each other.

Their love was undeniable, a bright flame that illuminated their lives, and everyone around them could see it. People noticed the way their eyes sparked with unspoken affection, how their voices softened when talking about one another, and the infectious energy that radiated from their connection. It was as if the world around them faded away, leaving just the two of them locked in a beautiful dance of emotion. But with that love came confusion; Lucy had never experienced such an intense bond with anyone before, and the thought of losing Jack was utterly unbearable. She was absolutely besotted, and she could sense that Jack felt the same way.

However, that sense of bliss was overshadowed by a creeping dread as the date of Jack's departure loomed closer. The upcoming party in July should have been a joyous occasion, but Lucy was haunted by the nagging feeling that Jack wouldn't return in time for their first dance. He had promised her that the trip would last around two weeks, but memories of his past trip to the Middle East lingered in her mind—those long, excruciating stretches of silence and waiting, where the days morphed into weeks. The thought of him being in Syria only intensified her anxiety, a whirlwind of fear and heartache spiralling within her. Why did she have to endure this torment repeatedly?

Finally, the day arrived when Jack would leave her side once more. As he packed up his belongings from her home, the sight of him folding his clothes and gathering his things made Lucy's heart ache. Each item he placed into his luggage felt like a piece of her being packed away too. They shared bittersweet phone calls amidst his long journey toward London, and despite the distance and anxiety, Jack's voice carried a soothing warmth. "I promise I'll make it back in time," he assured her, his words wrapping around her like a comforting embrace. Lucy clung to that reassurance, hoping that love would conquer the distance and time that now lay between them.

After an agonising wait of nearly 24 hours, Lucy received a message from Jack that sent a wave of relief washing over her. This time, he had made the bold decision to keep his phone, ensuring that they could stay connected despite the circumstances. The joy of hearing from him again brightened her day. Jack's message revealed that he was at an airport, waiting for his connecting flight to Syria, and he expressed his longing to hear her voice.

Their voices danced back and forth in the form of voice notes, filling the silences of his airport surroundings with intimacy and warmth. As Lucy listened, she could imagine the bustling atmosphere around him—the distant sounds of announcements, the soft rumble of luggage carts, and the hum of travellers moving along like a river flowing with anticipation. With every note from Jack, her heart felt a little lighter. This trip felt different; the palpable fear that had gripped her during his previous journey was gradually fading. Knowing that Jack had been permitted to keep his phone filled her with a reassuring sense that the dangers he faced were somehow diminished.

As her confidence grew, however, a shadow loomed when Jack's messages became sparse as his departure drew near. Lucy had expected this silence, understanding that the moments before a flight are often filled with preparation and anxiety, so she busied herself with daily life, trying to keep her mind occupied while awaiting his next contact.

Throughout his trip, Jack maintained a steady stream of communication, their conversations serving as a lifeline. There were moments when Lucy could hear the distant echoes of gunfire and shouts in the background, sending chills down her spine. Despite the chaos, Jack's calming voice always reassured her of his safety. "I'm tucked away, my girl," he would say, his words steady and confident, which gave Lucy a sense of comfort—even though worry gnawed at her. She found solace in the belief that he wouldn't risk their conversations if he were truly in danger. So, she clung to the conversations, determined to keep the connection alive until he told her he had to go.

Just days before the party that Lucy had been looking forward to, Jack delivered the exhilarating news: although the mission that had taken him overseas was still unfinished, he had been granted permission to fly back and join her for the celebration. It was thrilling news, yet it came with an undercurrent of intrigue; Jack had not been entirely forthcoming with his employers about his reasons for returning. Still, the fact that they had approved his leave filled Lucy with a bubbling excitement and hope for their time together. As she envisioned the party, anticipation turned into a palpable energy, making her heart race.

The day of the party finally arrived, infused with a sense of electric anticipation. Lucy stepped into the office, her heart racing as she pondered when Jack might arrive. She had no definite answer, as Jack hadn't given her a specific time and his messages had been sparse over the last day or so. She understood that he was flying back and likely didn't have the chance to communicate much, but each brief message she received—filled with declarations of his love and eagerness to see her—only heightened her excitement.

Determined to distract herself and make the day pass more quickly, Lucy threw herself into her work. The busier she kept, the faster the hours seemed to unfold. She meticulously organised her schedule, filling it with back-to-back appointments, hoping this would help the time slip away until she could be in Jack's arms again. As she moved through her tasks, Lucy's mind was often adrift in thoughts of him, imagining the moment they would finally reunite.

Just as she was leaving a client's home, the sound of her phone vibrating in her pocket broke through her thoughts. Glancing down, she noticed a missed call from Joanne, one of her colleagues who had opted to spend the day working from the office. Curiosity piqued, Lucy dialled her back, eager to hear what news Joanne had.

"Lucy! You missed quite the visit," Joanne exclaimed, her voice laced with excitement. "A very handsome—though a bit beaten up— man came looking for you earlier. He left a huge bouquet of flowers and a note."

The moment the words "handsome" and "man" left Joanne's lips, Lucy's heart skipped. She immediately recognised that it must be Jack, a smile spreading across her face at the thought of him. With a sudden surge of urgency, she rushed back to the office, her mind racing with visions of the vibrant flowers and the message he had left for her.

As she entered the office, her heart pounded in anticipation. The bouquet was likely a dazzling display of colours, a stark contrast to the dull office environment. She was determined to finish up her paperwork quickly so that she could track down Jack and bask in the glow of their long-awaited reunion. Lucy had never experienced such a rush of adrenaline. In the blink of an eye, she found herself darting around her cluttered office, hastily shoving her belongings into her handbag. Her heart raced as she called out cheerful goodbyes, her voice filled with excitement, before bolting for the door. All she could think about was seeing her charming Mr. Archer, though she had no idea exactly where he might be waiting for her.

Unbeknownst to her, Jack had been lurking in a dimly lit alleyway, his gaze fixed on her every move. He had planned to surprise her, his heart swelling with anticipation as he watched her enter and exit the office. Meanwhile, Lucy made her way toward the roadside where she had abandoned her weathered car. A sigh escaped her lips as she scanned the area, disappointment washing over her when she couldn't spot him.

At that moment, as she pressed the unlock button on her aging 4x4, Jack emerged from the shadows, a sly grin stretched across his face. He looked rugged and a bit worse for wear, dressed in combat trousers that clung to his strong legs, and a faded green t-shirt that showcased his impressive muscular arms. The golden brown tan he had acquired on his recent trip gave him a sun-kissed glow, making him look even more alluring.

Lucy gasped in surprise the moment their eyes locked, her excitement bubbling over as she sprinted toward him. Though Jack's usually pristine, shaven head and neatly groomed short beard were somewhat unruly, to Lucy, he was undeniably handsome. In that instant, all her worries melted away, and she was simply captivated by the man before her.

They stood in the sunlit street, enveloped in the warmth of each other's embrace, lips pressed softly together in a kiss that seemed to stretch into eternity. The world around them faded away as if time itself had paused, capturing the sheer joy of their reunion.

Lucy could hardly believe that Jack had actually made it back. Memories of his past broken promises flickered through her mind, leaving a tinge of scepticism lingering despite her excitement. She had braced herself to attend the party alone, but now, with him beside her, the thought felt utterly impossible. Her heart swelled with a tumult of relief and elation.

As they drove back, the atmosphere in the car shifted, filled with a blend of anticipation and trepidation. Jack started recounting the harrowing experiences he had faced while away, his voice steady but laced with the gravity of his words. He talked about a perilous situation where danger lurked at every corner—how shots rang out like thunder, echoing through the silence of the tense air, and how he had averted disaster to save someone ensnared in a hostile environment. Lucy listened, eyes wide and heart racing, as he painted vivid pictures with his tales of chaos and courage, of blasts that rumbled in the distance like ominous omens.

As he shared his story, Lucy felt a knot tighten in her stomach, a mix of dread and disbelief creeping over her. Mortification washed over her at the thought of Jack having to navigate such perilous scenarios. What if fate played a cruel joke and she lost him to that world? She found herself hanging on his every word, desperately seeking reassurance amidst the horror he described.

Though a part of her knew that some of his stories sounded far-fetched, as if plucked from an action movie, she tried to silence that inner doubt. After all, movies are often drawn from the depth of human experience and reality. Who was she to dismiss his truth? More than anything, what resonated within her was the fierce love she held for Jack, an emotion so profound that the very thought of a life without him felt unbearable, like a melody stripped of its most beautiful notes. She could only hope that their shared horizon was bright and free from shadows, full of laughter and love instead of chaos.

After spending a couple of hours getting ready together, the air was thick with laughter and the faint aroma of Lucy's favourite perfume and Jack's familiar aftershave, mingling with the sounds of a nearby DJ. They shared stories of the past few weeks, their voices occasionally melding into bursts of laughter that danced around the room. As the anticipation of the evening hung in the air, a creeping anxiety began to take hold of Lucy, one she had never experienced before.

Her mind was a whirlwind, consumed by the weight of everything Jack had confided in her. The memory of his daring escapades lingered like a shadow, and she couldn't help but question his choices. Why did he always seek out those perilous situations, veering away from the safety of their life together? What drove him to chase thrills, as if he were a moth drawn to an inescapable flame? Lucy, with her heart full of devotion, pondered whether she could ever offer him enough to quell that restless spirit.

As she stood in the bathroom in front of the mirror, adjusting her delicate earrings that sparkled like stars, she felt an ache deep within her. She knew, all too well, that this whirlwind romance was not sustainable in the long term. The electrifying joy of being reunited with Jack made her heart race, but beneath that excitement lay a gnawing realisation: a future with a man who thrived on uncertainty was a future ripe with worry and despair.

The thought of him disappearing into the abyss of danger made her insides twist in knots. He was handsome, with an effortless charm that swept her off her feet, treating her like some ethereal princess, yet uncertainty haunted her. Could she truly imagine a life where he would routinely vanish, risking everything, leaving her in a state of perpetual anxiety, heart pounding with the fear that he might not return?

She couldn't shake the feeling that his thirst for danger ran deeper than mere adrenaline; it felt like a chasm between them, one that she was terrified of crossing. The sparkle in his eyes when he spoke of his exploits contrasted sharply with the darkness swelling in her chest. Lucy found herself grappling with the unsettling notion that perhaps, despite all her efforts to anchor his adventurous heart, she might never be enough to tether him to a life that included her. For tonight at least, Lucy decided to push all of her anxieties and worries to the back of her mind and fully embrace the enchanting atmosphere around her.

The party was nothing short of magical, with twinkling fairy lights casting a warm glow over the room and laughter echoing like music. She walked in, hand in hand with Jack. They mingled effortlessly with the crowd, exchanging smiles and engaging in light-hearted conversations, their laughter ringing out as they danced beneath the shimmering disco ball. Each spin and sway brought them closer together, and stolen kisses felt electric, igniting a warmth that spread through Lucy's chest. She had never experienced such pure happiness before.

As the evening wore on, the air thick with camaraderie and celebration, they found themselves outside, a cool breeze wrapping around them. Here, with the stars overhead, they declared their love once more, words flowing like sweet nectar between them.

Upon returning to Lucy's home, they tossed aside their coats, their laughter echoing off the walls as they melted into the inviting softness of the sofa. Wrapped in each other's arms, the world outside faded away. Lucy took a deep breath, her voice tinged with sincerity as she confessed her struggles. "I want you to come and live with me," she said, her eyes searching his. "I get so anxious when you go away; I'm terrified that you won't come back, and that's something I simply can't live with."

Jack's gaze softened as he studied Lucy, love radiating from him like warmth from a fire. He leaned closer, his voice steady and reassuring. "I promise you; I'll make this my last trip. I'll ensure that I won't be assigned to anything else. I'll move in with you and start my life anew at your side."

Joy surged within Lucy at these words, filling her heart with a sense of relief and happiness for which she had longed. The future suddenly felt bright and filled with possibility, as they held onto each other, tightly woven as one amidst the comfort of their shared dreams.

The night together was amazing, their bodies entwined amidst a flurry of overwhelming emotion and exasperation. Their sex life had been amazing from the start but on this night, they melted into one. The adventure of new experiences, touching one another in various places, the use of blindfolds and handcuffs. They were resolute in their desire to end the night on a memorable note before Jack had to depart once more. The warmth of their bodies melded together, slick with sweat under the dim glow of the moonlight filtering through the curtains. Laughter and whispered secrets filled the air, igniting a spark between them that was impossible to ignore. Finally, exhaustion settled in, and they curled up together, limbs entwined like vines, finding comfort in the closeness. The soft rise and fall of their breaths synchronised, each inhalation and exhalation a silent promise, as they surrendered to the tranquillity of slumber, cocooned in the warmth of each other's embrace in the only way they knew how.

Chapter Fourteen

It had been a couple of weeks since that enchanting night when Lucy and Jack had first crossed the threshold into a deeper connection. Each day felt like a glorious adventure for Lucy as she revelled in the notion that Jack was about to move in. The anticipation bubbled within her—a delightful turmoil of excitement and nervous energy—as she daydreamed at her desk, her mind drifting far away from the usual office chat and the hum of fluorescent lights.

She envisioned the moment he would stand at her door, a smile brightening his face, with a suitcase in one hand and a cardboard box crammed full of his belongings in the other. The thought sent a warm flush through her; she imagined the embrace that would follow, the moment when he would finally be hers, enveloping her in an embrace that felt like coming home. The dreams continued to swirl in her mind, unfurling visions of a future she once thought was too distant to grasp—a wedding day, filled with laughter, love, and an abundance of joy.

Lucy couldn't help but share her affection for Jack with her friends. Her heart practically danced each time she spoke his name, her voice filled with warmth. There was a certain magic in the way she described him; each word painted a portrait of the beautiful man he was in her eyes, his kindness, charm, and charisma shining through. Yet, she found herself skirting around the details of his frequent trips away, leaving out the peculiar stories he had spun for her. Those tales felt too fantastical to share; she wished to preserve the image of Jack as the perfect partner, without the shadows of uncertainty creeping in from the outside world.

Lost in her thoughts, Lucy often found her mind wandering during work hours, each daydream drawing her further away from the clients and meetings that demanded her attention. On more than one occasion, her boss would pull her aside, concern etched on his face, to remind her to stay focused. Discontent brewed within her at the thought of being doubted, but the delightful images of Jack and their future together made it hard to stay grounded.

As Lucy journeyed home, the late afternoon sun casting a golden glow over everything, she was jarred from her daydreams by the sudden ringing of her phone. It was Jack on the line, his voice infused with excitement as he told her he was on his way—with all his belongings. The news sent a jolt of electricity through her veins. Jack was moving in for good, leaving behind the bustling streets of London, and she felt as though the universe had conspired in her favour.

Rushing through the door of her home, Lucy felt a surge of energy. She flung open drawers, clearing space for Jack's things with an eagerness that bordered on giddiness. She tidied the living room, adding small touches of warmth—fluffing cushions and lighting a few candles to create an inviting atmosphere. Everything needed to be perfect for the man who had turned her world upside down and inside out.

The next few weeks unfolded like a perfect bloom of blissful moments. Each day was filled with love and passion, a deep dedication to one another that enveloped Lucy and Jack. Their lives intertwined, creating a sanctuary of warmth and joy amidst the bustle of the outside world. Jack, radiant with enthusiasm, had landed a new job that ignited a spark within him. He could hardly contain his excitement as he recounted the details, his eyes glistening with the possibility of what lay ahead.

The prospect of a training course that would take him away for a few days had Jack buzzing with elation. He spoke animatedly about the new responsibilities he would hold—how he would become an investigator tasked with saving people from the brink of despair. Lucy listened, enraptured, her heart swelling with pride as she imagined her partner stepping into a role that would not only challenge him but also allow him to make a real difference in the lives of others. She projected into the future, hoping ardently that this opportunity would lead to a more stable home life for them, with Jack at home more often than not.

Once the training course concluded, Jack received his first assignment, and Lucy was overflowing with joy for him. As plans took shape, she envisioned a surprise visit to the hotel where he would be staying, dreaming of the delight on his face when she would show up unexpectedly to support him. She pictured the warm embrace they would share, the laughter that would fill the air as they relished each other's company, even if just for a brief moment.

The day arrived for Jack to start his new adventure. He meticulously packed his things, the anticipation buzzing around him like electricity. He cast a few fleeting glances toward Lucy, a mixture of sadness and excitement dancing in his gaze. "I'm going to miss you," he admitted softly, his voice tinged with genuine emotion, "but I can't wait for this new challenge." With a final lingering embrace, Jack stepped into the unknown, leaving behind sweet promises of reunions.

Jack had only been gone a few days, but for Lucy, each moment felt like an eternity. On her day off, she eagerly hopped into her car, the engine rumbling to life as she merged onto the busy motorway. The sun hung low in the sky, casting a warm golden glow on everything it touched, and the music blasted through the speakers, filling the car with vibrant melodies that matched the excitement fluttering in her chest.

As she drove, Lucy clutched her phone, her heart skipping a beat whenever it buzzed with a message from Jack. Each text was like a spark, lighting up her mood as he asked for updates on her journey, teasing her about how impatient he was to see her. She could almost picture him, pacing back and forth, a boyish grin on his face, his sparkling eyes reflecting the joy of their impending reunion. She longed to be back in his arms, cocooned in the warmth of his embrace, where all her worries melted away.

The ache of their separation nagged at her, the nights feeling longer without him by her side. She often found herself daydreaming about their moments together, imagining how blissful it would be to spend every waking hour wrapped up in his love, savouring the little things that made their bond unbreakable. Jack was perfect in her eyes—his kindness, charisma, and laughter filled every corner of her heart. She was resolute; no one else's opinion mattered.

As she pulled into the hotel car park, her heart soared at the thought of seeing him again. Just as she parked, her phone buzzed with a message: Jack was on his way down to reception. Excitement bubbled within her as she rushed inside, the scent of vanilla and the delicious smells coming from the food stands at the services where he was staying. The moment Jack stepped through the doors, his eyes shimmering with joy, Lucy felt her breath catch. He looked just as she remembered, his presence radiating warmth and happiness.

In that moment, surrounded by bustling travellers and the soft music in the lobby, Lucy knew that this was right. Jack was everything she had ever wanted, and she felt an unwavering certainty that nothing could ever change that. To her, he could do no wrong, and as she rushed into his waiting arms, she knew she was exactly where she belonged. Lucy and Jack climbed the narrow staircase to his new room, anticipation bubbling between them. As Jack swung open the door, Lucy stepped inside and took in her surroundings, her heart fluttering. The room was cosy and had a distinct personal touch—unlike the usual hotel rooms they had stayed in before. Sunlight streamed through the window, illuminating the mismatched furniture and giving the space a warm glow. Still, Lucy's thoughts were not on the decor, but rather on the joy of being reunited with Jack.

Without a moment's hesitation, they nestled onto the unmade bed, where the soft crumple of the sheets seemed to invite them in. They lost themselves in each other's arms, the afternoon light casting a golden haze as they made love, revelling in the comfort of their connection. Time slipped away, and hours blended into an intoxicating maze of happiness, their laughter echoing off the walls of the modest room.

Eventually, thoughts of coffee and sandwiches coaxed them out of their bliss. With hands intertwined, they sauntered to Lucy's car, still wrapped up in the warmth of their love. The drive to the local coffee shop was punctuated by easy conversation and playful glances, the thrill of being together propelling them forward. As they left, they encountered some of Jack's colleagues, who greeted him with friendly waves. Jack beamed with pride, effortlessly showcasing Lucy to his coworkers—a charming smile gracing his face as he introduced them.

Inside the coffee shop, the comforting aroma of freshly brewed coffee enveloped them. They settled into a little corner table, the clinking of cups and the hum of chatter creating a lively backdrop. Sipping their drinks, they dove deep into conversations about their dreams and aspirations—the future stretched before them like a blank canvas, waiting to be filled. Plans flowed freely as they discussed the possibility of moving to another country, their eyes sparkling with excitement. As Jack shared his hopes, Lucy felt a rush of affection, envisioning a life crafted together filled with endless love.

The next day, the sun shone over the landscape as Lucy prepared to leave once again. The trip had flown by like a fleeting dream, and now they faced the bitter reality of parting once more. Lucy's heart ached as she glanced at Jack, whose reassuring smile was a balm for her sadness. "It won't be long," he promised, his eyes sparkling with hope. Just one more week, he reminded her, until he completed his current placement. After that, he would be all hers until another opportunity whisked him away.

Lucy promised him she'd make one last visit, just for the day before Jack returned home. But for now, she had to face the mundane routine of her life without him. Jack would remain behind to immerse himself in his job, while Lucy would return to her own daily grind, each moment apart a reminder of the challenges their love faced. Despite the ache of separation, Lucy found solace in the transformation she witnessed in Jack; he radiated happiness now that he was engaged in work that fulfilled him.

The following week crawled by each day stretching on like a long, dreary winter. Lucy approached her routine with reluctance, shuffling into the office and returning home only to collapse into bed, her mind heavy with thoughts of Jack. The highlight of her days became the phone calls they shared—a lifeline that connected their hearts across the distance. Jack's regular video calls brightened her evenings, each glimpse of his face bringing a rush of warmth and affection.

"I need to see your beautiful face every day," he'd say, his voice filled with sincerity, and Lucy could feel the depth of his longing even through the screen. She revelled in these moments, feeling cherished in a way she had never experienced before. Most men simply didn't express their feelings like Jack did, and this made her feel as though she had unearthed a rare gem amid the ordinary. Each interaction made her heart swell with love, leaving her counting down the days until they could finally close the distance that separated them.

As Jack's return loomed closer, Lucy found herself perched anxiously on the edge of the couch, the soft fabric brushing against her skin but offering little comfort. The clock on the wall ticked loudly in the silence, each second amplifying her anticipation. She stared blankly at the phone, willing it to ring with the news that he was home and ready to be picked up.

In her mind, vivid recollections of their shared dreams danced like flickering candlelight—holidays at the beach, cosy nights wrapped in each other's arms, laughter echoing through their home. Yet, amidst the glow of these happy thoughts, a shadow of doubt crept in, dark and unwelcome. Jack's seemingly secretive demeanour weighed heavily on her heart like a stone. What truths lay hidden beneath the façade he presented to her?

Lucy loved Jack deeply; he was the sun in her sky, the pulse in her veins, the love of her life. Yet, she couldn't shake the feeling that something was amiss. One moment he was tender and attentive, wrapping her in warmth, and the next—he would withdraw, shrouded in a cloud of distance that left her feeling cold and alone. This erratic behaviour puzzled her and sent ripples of uncertainty coursing through her mind.

Jack had once mentioned, almost in passing, the unsavoury individuals tethered to his past—those to whom he felt an obligation, a debt that tied him in knots. He spoke of them with a caution that suggested more than mere acquaintance; they were dangerous, he'd said, and he warned her that they could turn their malice on her without a second thought if they deemed her a threat to their shadowy empire.

Over the months, Lucy had tried to compartmentalize these unsettling thoughts, burying them beneath the weight of her love for Jack. But now, as the shadows lengthened around her, they surged forth—insistent and demanding her attention.

Resolute, she resolved that when Jack finally crossed the threshold of their home, she would muster the courage to confront him. She would delve deeper, seeking answers about the demons that lingered in his past. Deep within her heart, she clung to the hope that he had left that life behind, but another, quieter part of her sensed that the ties were not so easily severed. The pull of his past felt omnipresent, and it was time for her to uncover the truth, no matter how unsettling it might be.

As the sun began to dip below the horizon, casting shadows over the landscape, Lucy received the eagerly awaited call that Jack was on his way to the coach station. An electric mix of anticipation and anxiety surged through her as she jumped into her car, her heart racing with the thought of him returning. A cascade of memories washed over her; each one tinged with the nagging worry of Jack's dark past. Would he finally open up about the shadows that loomed behind him?

She pulled in close to the station, her mind a whirl of questions. Lucy knew that she had to tread lightly in her pursuit of the truth, careful not to frighten him away with her curiosity. Each detail she had learned so far cast a long shadow, but deep down, she felt she could trust him completely. After all, Jack had never given her any reason to doubt his sincerity.

The sight of him approaching sent her heart soaring. Jack's striking features were illuminated by the soft light of dusk, his rucksack casually slung over one shoulder. Clutched in his hands was an exuberant bouquet of vibrant flowers, their colours a vivid contrast against the fading day. As he strolled toward her car, his face broke into a radiant smile that seemed to brighten the entire station.

When he reached the passenger side, he leaned in without a moment's hesitation, capturing her lips in a long, tender kiss that sent a thrill through her. It felt as if time had stopped, the world around them fading away, leaving just the two of them in their own bubble of warmth and connection. After a moment that felt both fleeting and eternal, Jack tossed his bag into the boot and slid into the seat beside her.

"Oh my god, I've missed you!" he exclaimed, his eyes sparkling with genuine joy.

"I've missed you too!" Lucy replied, her voice barely above a whisper as she took in the familiar, beloved features of the man she cared for deeply. They embraced; a comforting interlude that helped ease the tension in Lucy's chest.

As they drove home, the conversation flowed effortlessly, touching on the mundane details of work and the trivial happenings of life. Yet beneath the surface of their light banter, Lucy could feel the weight of unasked questions pressing down on her. The desire to uncover the hidden facets of Jack's life lingered in her mind like a poignant melody, growing louder with each passing moment. She needed to know what secrets he held, almost turning the revelation of his past into a personal quest, one she felt compelled to pursue despite the risks.

Once they arrived home, the familiar warmth of their connection took over them, and Lucy found herself swept away, the carefully planned conversation with Jack slipping from her mind. The following days were like a dream—every stolen glance and shared smile only deepened the love they had found in one another. Lucy couldn't shake the shadow of Jack's past that flickered in her thoughts, a looming spectre she hesitated to confront. What if they could build a future without unravelling the tangled threads of his history? She knew, deep down, that the gnawing curiosity would eventually claw its way to the surface. But for now, as they basked in the blissful perfection of their life together, she decided to let it be.

One evening, with the glow of the television dimmed and the room bathed in soft shadows, they nestled on the couch. The bustling sounds of the outside world faded away as Jack took her feet into his hands, gently massaging away the tension of Lucy's long day. The air was thick with intimacy, and it was then that Jack, with a deep breath that seemed to carry the weight of his past, began to share his story—one he had chosen to unveil without her prompting.

He painted a vivid picture of his life before— a turbulent whirlpool where he found himself ensnared by drug dealers and foreign groups. Jack spoke of betrayal and survival, recounting how these ruthless individuals had pulled him from the jaws of death, leaving an indelible mark on his soul. His voice trembled as he revealed that he owed them a debt; they were the ones who had helped him forge a new existence in a world that had otherwise written him off. Lucy listened, captivated and horrified, as he recounted the harrowing memories of watching people he cared for spiral into darkness, some even succumbing to their despair.

The air felt thick with the weight of his revelations, and Lucy's heart raced with shock and empathy. She had her own shadows lurking in her past, secrets she had buried deep and rarely shared. But in this moment of raw vulnerability from Jack, she felt an unspoken bond—a sense of obligation to share a part of her own history. The confession stirred within her, begging to be released.

Jack's stories flowed, detailing not just the dangers of his past, but the chilling reality of weaponry and information that became his currency for survival. He assured Lucy, almost pleadingly, that he had not recently crossed the line into illegality, mindful of her concerns, which she had voiced more than once. But the depth of his experience left her feeling both fortunate and frightened. In the stillness of the evening, as his fingers kneaded her feet, Lucy recognised the profound trust and vulnerability that had woven them even closer together amidst the shadows of their pasts.

Over the next few weeks, Jack began to unveil stories that left Lucy reeling, each revelation more shocking than the last. His voice was low and intense as he detailed the perilous situations he faced while working for the government, painting vivid pictures of high-stake operations in dangerous corners of the world. Lucy could almost feel the palpable tension in the air he described a tension that gripped her heart with a mixture of fear and fascination.

Every word he spoke sent her mind spiralling into a chaotic swirl of emotions. Deep down, a nagging sense of caution gnawed at her, whispering that perhaps the safest path would be to walk away from this man who had so thoroughly captivated her heart. But the thought of a life devoid of Jack felt unbearable, a world of loneliness that loomed large before her.

She grappled with the unsettling truth that some of Jack's stories didn't quite align with reality. Despite the flickering doubts in her mind, she found herself willing to overlook the shadows of dishonesty that danced around his words. He had a way of looking at her, the warmth in his gaze a balm for her unease, as he insisted that his lies were born of a desire to protect her. "Some things I can't share, Lucy," he confessed, his voice heavy with gravity. "If I did, the consequences could be dire—prison, or worse, depending on who got this information."

With every new narrative, Lucy felt as if her world was fracturing, the pieces scattering like shards of glass. "I'm not a good person, Lucy!" Jack exclaimed; his anguish palpable as he bared more of his troubled past. She was taken aback, struggling to reconcile the kind, gentle man before her with the turbulent figure lurking in his stories. "I don't understand!" she urged, her voice trembling with disbelief. "You're so lovely with me—how can you be capable of such madness?"

As Jack's secrets unfolded like a dark, twisted tale, the horrifying possibility loomed in her mind: could it be that people had perished at the hands of the man she adored? The gravity of it all, the juxtaposition of Jack's sweetness with the chaos of violence he casually recounted, left Lucy in turmoil, her heart caught in a tempest of love and fear. She felt utterly lost, trying to navigate through the storm that was Jack's reality, and her own desperate need to believe in the goodness she saw in him.

Jack swore to Lucy, his voice laced with a mix of urgency and assurance, that he had requested to leave the clutches of his enigmatic government employer, and astonishingly, they had accepted his request. Lucy struggled to believe it had been so simple, but deep down, a nagging intuition whispered that this was merely the surface of a much deeper narrative—one that might not signify an end to their tribulations or herald the new beginning she desperately longed for. All Lucy craved was a serene life with her strikingly charming man, yet doubt gnawed at her—had she unwittingly chosen the wrong partner in her quest for tranquillity?

Since Jack had moved in, Lucy found herself wholly absorbed in his world, shifting her focus away from her friends and family. The once vibrant connections that filled her life began to fade like distant echoes, leaving only Jack as her primary confidant. She had always relied on a network of loved ones to help her navigate life's challenges, but the weight of the secrets Jack had entrusted to her felt heavy on her shoulders, leaving her bound to him in ways that felt both exhilarating and suffocating. It was a peculiar dichotomy—to feel so close to someone while simultaneously holding them at arm's length with unshared truths.

Lucy couldn't shake the feeling that there were shadows lurking around Jack, a darkness she couldn't quite grasp. She often pondered the mystery behind his injuries—how could a man so sweet, generous, and charming return home with bruises and scrapes as if the world itself conspired to trip him up? Jack always brushed off her concerns with a casual smile, attributing his wounds to minor accidents—a bump into a doorframe or a misstep on the pavement. Although these explanations seemed plausible, they felt increasingly inadequate to Lucy. After all, he was a newcomer to the area; who could possibly hold a grudge against a charming, kind-hearted man like Jack?

Yet, as the days turned into weeks and the pattern of injuries continued, Lucy's suspicions began to deepen into a gnawing fear. What if the truth was entangled in the very secrets that bound them together? As her heart yearned for the simplicity she once embraced, she wrestled with the thought that the man she loved might be entwined in a web of danger she could scarcely imagine.

Lucy embarked on her mission to uncover the truth about Jack, her heart racing with both determination and trepidation. She was acutely aware that she had crossed a line by sneaking into his private digital world, but the gnawing need for answers clouded her judgment. Jack had been on her computer, and she had discovered his usernames and how to recover the passwords hidden beneath layers of digital security. Her fingers hesitated for just a moment before she pressed the keys, pushing aside the nagging guilt that accompanied her every thought.

As she logged into Jack's email account, the screen flickered to life, revealing a web of correspondence that sent chills down her spine. Among the myriad messages, emails from Sara, Jack's ex-girlfriend, stood out like a beacon. Jack had insisted that he and Sara had parted ways long before Lucy came into the picture, but the evidence before her painted a very different picture. Receipts for gifts, meticulously listed and dated, spoke volumes; it seemed that Jack's version of their relationship was a carefully constructed facade.

Jack had often recounted tales of his past with Sara, cloaked in a shroud of danger and intrigue. He had warned Lucy that Sara hailed from a menacing family entrenched in a notorious crime network, asserting that he was at constant risk. "They'd kill me if they had the chance," he had said, his voice grave, eyes darting furtively as though the mere mention of her name would invoke their wrath. Now, Lucy felt a swell of disbelief and confusion rise within her as she scanned the screen.

The emails were an intimate narrative of their interaction—Sara beckoning him to join her at social gatherings, discussing favours that she had obtained for him, and weaving the threads of connection that Jack had so insistently claimed were severed. Why, in his attempts to distance himself, was Jack engaging in this clandestine correspondence? The contrast between his words and the digital evidence was stark and unsettling.

With every click, Lucy felt the weight of betrayal settle heavily on her shoulders. She knew she had to confront Jack the moment he returned from his assignment. The days without him had stretched on, the silence between them palpable, and his uncharacteristically infrequent communication gnawed at her insides. What was he hiding, and could the revelations about Sara's continued presence in his life explain his growing distance? Lucy's mind whirled with questions, fuelled by a blend of fear and resolve. She had to get to the bottom of this; the truth, no matter how painful, was something she couldn't ignore any longer.

Over the coming days, as Jack's return drew nearer, Lucy felt a growing knot of anxiety tightening in her chest. The sensation seeped into every corner of her life, casting a shadow over her workdays and draining her enthusiasm. Her boss, concerned about her state, pulled her into the office multiple times, his voice laced with worry as he asked if she was okay. Each inquiry felt like a piercing reminder of her unravelling state of mind. Lucy sensed that she was teetering on the brink of collapse, her composure cracking under the weight of uncertainty.

What she craved most was Jack's presence—a calming balm for her frayed nerves. Yet, each passing day intensified her emotional turmoil, turning her anxious thoughts into a simmering anger, not directed at Jack, but at her boss. Frustrations bubbled to the surface, manifesting in sharp words and irritated snaps whenever he checked in on her. Inside, she felt as if she were caught in a trap, desperately seeking refuge in the warm embrace of Jack's reassuring love.

Despite the physical distance that separated them, Jack diligently sent her loving messages each day, words meant to bridge the gap. Yet, with each text, Lucy felt more isolated, a creeping sense of rejection settling in her heart like a cold stone. Her mind became consumed by the troubling discovery of emails that gnawed at her confidence in their relationship.

One night, the tension reached a breaking point during a phone call with Jack. The floodgates opened, and she blurted out what had been weighing heavily on her: the emails from Sara. Jack's response was immediate but evasive. He insisted that the emails weren't from Sara, that the address was cleverly disguised to mislead anyone checking them. They were confidential communications from his government employer, he explained, and he promised that one day he would teach her the coding necessary to decipher the messages herself. Trust him, he urged, assuring her that he would never betray her heart.

Yet Lucy struggled to accept his words. Her mind raced with doubt as she recalled the intimate pictures embedded within the emails—images of Sara smiling, almost mockingly. If those emails were indeed from Jack's employer, then why would they contain such personal snapshots? The questions spiralled, leaving her feeling more confused and betrayed.

When Jack finally returned home, he seemed to melt the anxiety away with his warm, kind presence. He swept her into a comforting embrace, making her feel cherished and valued once more, as though the world righted itself in his arms. They spent precious moments together, Jack showering her with affection that made her heart swell. In the comforting glow of their reunion, Lucy made a conscious decision— she would choose to believe in Jack's assurances. After all, love forged a powerful bond, one that she was determined to protect, even as doubt lingered at the edges of her thoughts.

During Jack's time at home, he became a regular visitor to Lucy's office, often surprising her with an array of beautiful flowers and extravagant gifts that he presented with a flourish before her colleagues. Each time he entered her office, the atmosphere seemed to shift, filled with a sweet, floral scent and excitement. Lucy's heart would flutter at the sight of him; he brought a sparkle to her day that made her feel incredibly special. While she didn't quite understand the need for such lavish tokens of affection—after all, her love for him did not hinge on material gifts—she couldn't deny the pleasure it brought her to be spoiled in front of her peers.

Her colleagues, however, began to whisper among themselves, expressing concern over Jack's actions. They found his displays excessive and somewhat obsessive. Yet, Lucy, caught in the warm glow of her infatuation, dismissed their murmurs as jealousy. "They're just envious that their partners aren't doing the same," she thought, brushing off the unease that seemed to hang in the air like a heavy fog. Though she listened to their words, Jack utterly captivated her. To her, he was a charming prince who could do no wrong, and his intentions seemed purely rooted in love.

But the whispers amplified when it came to Jack's other behaviours. He had started calling her office after dropping her off, checking in to see if she was settled in for the day. Rumours of him sitting in his car for hours outside the building dotted the conversations around the water cooler, sparking further concern among her colleagues. Did they not see that Jack was simply being protective, wanting to ensure her safety? These thoughts reassured Lucy, who decided to discount any claims that he might be crossing the line into possessiveness or control.

One crisp afternoon, as they took a leisurely drive under a sun-dappled sky, Jack broached a subject that set Lucy's heart racing. "If you could go anywhere in the world for a short trip, where would it be?" he asked casually, his eyes glinting with curiosity. Without hesitation, Lucy replied, "Iceland, to see the northern lights!" The thought of those shimmering colours dancing across the night sky had always captivated her imagination. When Jack inquired, "Why?" her answer flowed easily.

"Oh, no reason!" he said, a playful smile dancing across his lips as he swiftly turned the conversation to lighter topics. But remnants of his question lingered in the air, leaving Lucy with a tantalising sense that perhaps Jack was planning something special for the future.

The following week at work, Lucy found herself enveloped in a whirlwind of activity. The demands of her new role consumed her, and the persistent thoughts of Jack faded to the background, replaced by a flurry of tasks and responsibilities. She had recently acquired a batch of new clients and was fiercely determined to make a lasting impression on each one. The absence of Jack, who was away on business, felt less daunting against the backdrop of her busy schedule.

Every night, without fail, Jack would call her from afar, and the warmth of his voice resonated deeply. Their conversations were filled with love and affection, a delightful exchange of heartfelt compliments that left them both feeling elated and uplifted. In those moments, Lucy felt certain she had found the man of her dreams—even if he remained, for the most part, a charming enigma.

One particularly hectic afternoon, while sitting at her desk surrounded by a cascade of paperwork and the echo of office chatter, Lucy noticed an incoming email to her personal account. Curious, she opened it, but soon realised it was from a car hire company that didn't appear to be based in England. A wave of intrigue washed over her, and despite her initial resolve to ignore it, she found herself unable to resist the pull of curiosity.

After grappling with her thoughts for about an hour, she returned to the email, scanning the text with heightened anticipation. Her heart raced as she discovered that the company was located in Iceland, and even more astonishing was the detail that a car had been hired for a date just a few weeks away. A thrill of disbelief coursed through her veins. She could hardly comprehend it. Jack was undeniably romantic, and the idea of him planning something so adventurous left her breathless with excitement. The revelation felt like a whisper of love, hinting at a surprise waiting just beyond the horizon.

After finishing her shift at the bustling office, Lucy felt a flutter of anticipation in her chest. Deep down, she had vowed to keep the thrilling surprise Jack had planned under wraps; she didn't want to spoil the mystery he had crafted for her. The moment she stepped outside into the crisp evening air, her phone buzzed with a familiar ringtone. It was Jack.

As soon as he realised his error in sending the receipt for the car hire to her email, a pang of concern washed over him. He knew all too well that Lucy's curiosity often led her to uncover hidden surprises. When he questioned her about it, Lucy hesitated, a tiny pang of guilt surfacing. Despite her best efforts to mask her excitement, she eventually succumbed, her voice bursting with joy as she confessed that she had indeed spotted the car rental details.

Jack's heart sank for a moment, wishing he could have unveiled the magical trip to Iceland in a spectacular way. However, the sheer delight radiating from Lucy's words transformed his disappointment into pure joy. Every syllable she spoke, dripping with excitement, fuelled his own thrill. They could now share in the joy of planning their adventure together, discussing the breathtaking landscapes, hot springs, and the mesmerising Northern Lights that awaited them. Jack knew Lucy dreamed of visiting Iceland, but witnessing her euphoric response was more gratifying than he could have imagined.

As the weeks rushed by in a flurry of anticipation, they found themselves submerged in preparations for their unforgettable journey. Buying thermal clothing became a cherished activity—each soft layer of fabric and vibrant colour igniting visions of snow-covered mountains and shimmering glaciers. Just a couple of days remained before they would embark on their adventure, and their home was a delightful chaos of packed bags, travel guides, and Icelandic maps.

Lucy could hardly contain her excitement; the thrill of exploring a new land filled her with uncontainable joy. More than the destination itself, she longed for the precious moments they would share— uninterrupted by daily life, filled only with laughter, exploration, and the romance of wandering hand in hand through the wild, untouched beauty of Iceland.

Chapter Fifteen

A turbulent day had culminated in the dawn of Lucy and Jack's eagerly anticipated flight to Iceland. As they stood at the threshold of their home before heading to the airport hotel for their early morning journey, a wave of panic washed over Jack. He suddenly turned to Lucy; his brow furrowed with concern and announced that he couldn't find his passport. A cold chill of dread engulfed them as they tore through every corner of their home—the bookshelf, the kitchen drawers, even the laundry basket—but it seemed to have vanished into thin air. She felt as if her dreams of exploring the ethereal landscapes of Iceland were being crushed under the weight of reality. Devastated, she slumped onto the sofa, tears brimming in her eyes, ready to give up on their adventure.

Just then, Jack burst into the room, a wide grin splitting his face. Laughing heartily, he wrapped her in his warm embrace, reassuring her not to be so dramatic. He reached into his rucksack and triumphantly produced his passport, the very object that had sent them into a tailspin. He had packed it there all along, blissfully unaware when he'd first checked. Relief flooded back into Lucy's heart, and a shared laughter echoed through the room, replacing the earlier anxiety. They quickly gathered their things and set off, excitement bubbling beneath the surface as they began their journey, the first step being their stay at the airport hotel.

The journey to the hotel had drained them both—each step filled with anticipation yet marked by the fatigue of the day's earlier treks. As they entered their hotel room, they melded into each other, curling up in a comfortable pile of blankets. The room was dimly lit, and a soft glow from the streetlights outside shadows of them across the room. They fell into a dreamy state, nestled together, hearts fluttering with joy for the adventures that lay ahead.

At 5 a.m., the shrill sound of the alarm pierced through their slumber, awakening them from their idyllic dreams for their 6:30 a.m. flight. For a moment, they both groaned, reluctant to leave the warmth of the bed. But as the reality of potentially missing their flight sank in, they quickly rallied.

The taxi ride to the airport was filled with excitement, the streets still dim and quiet. Arriving at the airport, they effortlessly glided through security, buoyed by adrenaline, and soon found themselves in the lively departure lounge. The aroma of fresh coffee and warm breakfast rolls wafted through the air, enticing them to indulge.

As they settled at a little table, Lucy's fingers danced over her phone, searching through the internet to discover the hidden gems they could explore in Iceland. Jack, seated across from her, couldn't help but smile at the spark in her eyes; it was an infectious enthusiasm that made his heart swell. Having travelled extensively, Jack had become accustomed to the thrill of exploring new places, yet witnessing Lucy's enchantment at the prospect of traveling beyond the UK reignited a spark of adventure within him.

Reaching across the table, Jack took Lucy's hands in his, their fingers intertwined in a gesture of affection. Looking into her eyes, he softly told her just how much he loved her. At that moment, Lucy felt as though she were floating—completely cherished and adored. This was the life she had long envisioned, and here was the man she had dreamed of sharing it with.

The flight seemed to take no time at all as Lucy and Jack talked about the future and the amazing adventures they would have. They had so many plans that a lifetime just didn't seem enough. They had already made journey's together but nothing this big. This was the biggest adventure yet. Jack seemed to be a bit nervous about something, but Lucy couldn't quite get out of him what that was. She knew he had planned something, but he wasn't giving anything away. Lucy soon forgot about her suspicions when they landed in Reykjavik though. It was freezing cold, but she didn't care.

Jack arranged and dealt with everything when they got there, and Lucy had no idea what was going on. Next thing she knew they were being led outside to a large car ready for them to drive off in. They got in the car and headed off to the hotel. Jack drove with confidence. Lucy had been nervous about driving on the other side of the road which jack had found cute, so he agreed to do the driving while they were there. As they pulled into the carpark at the hotel Lucy looked at the beautiful huge building in front of her. They strolled into the lobby, where the polished marble floors gleamed under the soft glow of chandeliers, casting intricate shadows across the room. Glass cabinets lined the walls, showcasing a dazzling array of artifacts that whispered stories of history and culture, each piece a testament to craftsmanship and time.

Taking the lift up to their floor, anticipation swirled between them. When the doors slid open, they stepped into an elegant corridor that led to their suite. Upon entering, Lucy gasped softly. The suite was a masterpiece, boasting a harmonious blend of luxury and comfort. An inviting office area, plush seating arrangement, and two exquisitely designed bathrooms framed a massive bedroom that was nothing short of opulent. Rich fabrics draped across the furniture, and the soft neutral colours of the decor exuded warmth. Lucy couldn't believe the effort that Jack had gone to; a flutter of joy filled her heart. His desire to make her happy shone brightly through each thoughtfully arranged element of their stay, and her heart swelled with gratitude.

After thoroughly exploring their breathtaking suite, they decided to embark on a journey to discover the area. They drove along winding roads, the car gliding over hills and valleys, each turn revealing more of the stunning landscape. The sun dipped lower in the sky, casting a golden glow over the scenery as it began to set, painting the world in shimmering oranges and soft pinks. Jack eased the car to a stop in a tranquil lay-by that overlooked a vast, sparkling lake, the surface glistening like a blanket of diamonds beneath the fading sunlight.

Towering hills of ancient volcanic rock framed the lake, their rugged beauty forming a stunning backdrop.

Both of them stepped out of the car, their breath visible in the crisp evening air. Jack took Lucy's hand and led her gently down a path carved into the dark, rocky hillside. As Lucy stood atop the volcanic landscape, mesmerized by the tranquil expanse of the lake before her, she could feel the magic of the moment enveloping them. Jack fumbled in his pockets; his excitement palpable. "What are you looking for?" Lucy asked, a playful smile dancing on her lips. "Just hang on!" replied Jack, a hint of mystery in his voice.

Finally, he pulled something out of his pocket and turned to Lucy, his eyes glinting with mischief and affection. "There's a reason I brought you here, Lucy!" he said, and in that moment, the world around them faded away, leaving only the promise of a beautiful surprise and the warmth of their connection beneath the twilight sky.

At that moment, Jack walked toward Lucy, a small velvet box cradled in his hand, his heart pounding with anticipation. The sun dipped low on the horizon, casting a shadows all around them as he approached. "You once said you wanted to be with me forever, Lucy. Did you mean that?" he asked, his voice tinged with vulnerability.

"Of course I did!" replied Lucy, her eyes sparkling with excitement. The world seemed to fade, leaving just the two of them in their own bubble of joy.

In an instant, Jack's demeanour shifted as he lowered himself onto one knee, the rock beneath him gently crumbling. Lucy's heart raced; could this truly be happening? Jack looked up at her, his gaze steady yet brimming with a mix of hope and nerves. He opened the box, revealing a beautiful but subtle diamond engagement ring that glimmered softly in the fading light, reflecting the depth of their love.

"Will you marry me?" he asked, his voice a mixture of anticipation and apprehension.

Lucy felt a rush of emotions crash over her like a tidal wave. She was momentarily taken aback, fumbling in her pockets as nervousness surged within her. She knew the answer she wanted to give, but words momentarily escaped her. Jack's eyes flickered with uncertainty, but just as doubt began to cloud the moment, she found her voice, strong and clear. "Of course I will!" she exclaimed, her voice filled with pure joy.

Jack sprang up, and in an instant, they were wrapped in each other's arms, the world around them dissolving into a backdrop. Giggling nervously, Jack said, "I was a little worried for a second there!"

They stood entwined, taking in the breathtaking scenery—vibrant autumn leaves beneath a sky painted with streams of pink and purple. The air was crisp, fragrant with the earthy scent of nature, and the moment felt almost magical, as if time had stopped just for them.

After a few moments, they returned to the warmth of their car, their hearts still dancing with exhilaration. As they drove through the picturesque countryside, the windows rolled down to let the cool breeze swirl around them, they talked animatedly about their engagement, dreams, and what the future might hold.

Each shared vision brought them closer, forming a story of hopes and aspirations that seemed seamlessly intertwined. Everything felt perfect, from the laughter echoing in the car to the quaint landscape framing their journey.

By the time they returned to the hotel, they were completely in love, their hearts aglow with promise and possibility, basking in the warmth of what they had just committed to—a lifetime together.

Jack had shared his heartfelt intentions with Lucy during their journey, revealing that he had meticulously planned to propose later in their trip. Yet, the moment was so precious and exhilarating that he could hardly contain himself. When they arrived at the serene lake, surrounded by breathtaking landscapes and kissed by the glow of the northern lights, he felt an irresistible urge to make the moment unforgettable.

As they returned to their beautiful hotel room after a day filled with exploration, the evening air hinted at romance. They slipped beneath the warm covers, drawing close to each other and sharing smiles and intimate touches that spoke volumes. In that tender moment, Lucy felt as if she were caught in a beautiful dream from which she never wanted to awaken, wrapped in the warmth of Jack's arms.

The next morning dawned with the promise of new adventures. They rose with enthusiasm, ready to seize the day, and soon found themselves wandering into a charming local shopping centre. There, nestled between shops, they discovered a quaint little coffee shop, its inviting aroma wrapping around them like a warm blanket. They settled into a little corner table, where hours slipped away as they engrossed themselves in heartfelt conversations.

Though they had yearned to visit the famous blue lagoon hot springs, fate had different plans as it was fully booked. Undeterred, they sought out an alternative destination and agreed that the journey would be worthwhile. They picked out suitable swimwear, their laughter bubbling over as they envisioned the experience ahead.

As evening began to fall, they arrived at the hot springs, where steam rose gently from the water, creating an ethereal atmosphere. Each entered their respective changing rooms, the excitement palpable in the air. Once ready, they met again and stepped into the inviting waters, feeling the contrast of the chilly evening air against the warm embrace of the springs.

Surrounded by the beauty of nature, they found themselves in pools of varying temperatures, their laughter mingling with the soothing sounds of water. As the sun slipped beneath the horizon, Jack suddenly pointed skyward. Lucy's gaze shifted upwards, where the night sky revealed a breathtaking display of the northern lights. The vibrant greens unfurled like a celestial curtain, dancing in harmony with the peaceful surroundings.

They settled together in the hot water, the warmth encircling them, while above, the northern lights wove an enchanting dance across the sky. Everything felt magical, a perfect culmination of love, adventure, and the beauty of the moment they were sharing. It was a memory they would cherish forever, a perfect addition to their remarkable journey together.

On their final day, they made their way back to the quaint little coffee shop where they had first experienced the joy of that magical moment. The sun filtered gently through the large windows, pouring onto the rustic wooden tables adorned with small vases of vibrant flowers. They settled into their favourite corner, the aroma of freshly brewed coffee all around them like a comforting embrace.

As they sipped their lattes, rich and creamy with just the right hint of sweetness, they spent hours lost in conversation, bringing together their hopes, dreams, and aspirations. The air buzzed with excitement as they shared ideas and laughter, each story igniting a spark of inspiration in the other. They reminisced about their adventures, pausing occasionally to soak in the atmosphere and the chatter of other patrons, which only added to the ambiance of this cherished spot.

As the day wore on, a bittersweet feeling began to settle in. They were acutely aware this would be their last moments in this place, and the thought of leaving brought a wave of sadness. Yet, intertwined with that sorrow was a profound happiness, knowing they were carrying home a treasure trove of hope and inspiration.

Eventually, they gathered their things, reluctant to part from the cosy refuge of the coffee shop. After returning their car, they made their way to the airport, the bustling atmosphere heightening their sense of adventure. As they approached the terminal, they exchanged glances filled with contentment, feeling as if life had woven them into a perfect tapestry of experiences, leaving them utterly fulfilled and eager for what lay ahead.

Back at home, Lucy could hardly contain her excitement as she burst through the front door, eager to share the mesmerizing tale of her recent adventures. She swiftly picked up her phone and called Dale, her voice bubbling with enthusiasm as she began to unravel the magical story of how she got engaged.

Dale was taken aback, his eyes widening in surprise. Lucy's engagement had always seemed like a distant dream—something she had vehemently rejected in the past. He couldn't help but feel a mix of astonishment and concern. But as Lucy shared the details, it became clear that this was a different chapter in her life. Jack was no ordinary man; he was the embodiment of her dreams. She spoke with fervour about him, wrapped in the warmth of love that radiated from her every word.

Jack was everything she had longed for—romantic, thoughtful, and attentive. With each heartfelt gesture, he changed Lucy's world. She described the vibrant bouquets of flowers he would bring her, their colours vivid against the backdrop of her mundane days. His compliments danced like whispers on the wind, lifting her spirit higher than she had ever thought possible. And then there was that unforgettable moment under the northern lights, where he knelt before her in the soft glow of the auroras, a ring in his hand that sparkled like the stars above.

Lucy revelled in the memories of their shared trips, each one an adventure that solidified her belief that Jack was her soulmate. He was her anchor during the storms of life, always ready to lift her spirits when she felt down. Whenever she sought reassurance, his gentle words were a balm to her soul, rich with sincerity and emotion. "I love you," he would say, and with each proclamation, she felt a warmth envelop her heart.

As Lucy continued to unravel her story, Dale listened intently, the initial surprise melting away into understanding. He could see the radiance in her eyes, the glow of happiness that surrounded her like a soft embrace. Sincerely happy for his sister, he congratulated her, recognizing that the joy shining from her was what truly mattered. He had never seen her this blissful before, and although doubts lingered about Jack, his sister's happiness was paramount to him.

Later, the siblings shared the news with their parents. Lucy got to relive the beautiful tale once more, her heart swelling with affection. It felt as if she was the protagonist in a romance novel, living a story with dreams and love. Her parents beamed with pride and joy, offering their warm congratulations, their support reassuring her already perfect story.

With a heart full of elation, Lucy turned to social media to announce her engagement to the world. The moment she clicked "post," a wave of congratulations flooded in from friends and family both near and far, each message lighting up her screen like fireworks. As she read each heartfelt comment, she couldn't help but feel like the luckiest girl alive, radiant with the knowledge that she was embarking on a new chapter filled with love, adventure, and bliss.

Over the next few months, Jack and Lucy found themselves wrapped in the warmth of their love as they diligently planned their future together, with stars in their eyes and a shared vision for their dream wedding. They envisioned a picturesque beach wedding or a romantic lakeside ceremony in the enchanting landscapes of Italy. While the allure of the Maldives danced in their imaginations, they knew that bringing their beloved family and friends to such a distant paradise might prove challenging. Thus, they settled on the idea of a wedding by one of Italy's famous lakes, surrounded by breathtaking scenery and the gentle rustle of the breeze.

Their days were filled with excitement as they consulted experienced wedding planners, diving into discussions about budgets, floral arrangements, and the perfect venue. Lucy, with her infectious enthusiasm, managed to gather her family for a cherished moment after discovering the wedding dress of her dreams. The experience was surreal, and the anticipation bubbled inside her as Jack encouraged, "Just buy it. It's what you want, so you should have it, and you will look absolutely beautiful in it."

With her heart racing, Lucy attended the dress fitting accompanied by her mum, friends, and the ever-supportive Dale. She twirled in front of the mirror, trying on a variety of dresses, but none captured her heart quite like the exquisite gown she had first seen shimmering in the boutique window as she drove past. It was a vision of elegance and beauty – a perfect reflection of her dreams for that special day. In a moment of pure joy, Lucy sent a picture of herself in the enchanting dress to Jack. His immediate and heartfelt response echoed her own feelings—he agreed, wholeheartedly, that it was indeed the right dress, a flawless choice that left them both buzzing with anticipation for their future.

As Christmas approached, the air filled with festivity and the promise of new beginnings. Jack, who usually found little joy in the holiday season, set aside his reservations for Lucy's sake. Their shared moments felt like magic as they exchanged the thoughtfully chosen gifts, they had picked out for one another. Lucy presented Jack with a bracelet that held profound significance, engraved with the date of their engagement, their names, and a charming picture of them together in the steaming hot springs. It symbolized a connection that transcended the ordinary, a token of love that he would carry with him always. Jack's eyes lit up, filled with warmth and gratitude as he kissed her, moved by her thoughtfulness.

After the New Year festivities faded, both Jack and Lucy reluctantly returned to the rhythms of their work lives. Jack, with his suitcase in hand, had to leave for another long stint, while Lucy prepared to navigate the bustling office once more. As she sat at her desk, her mind drifted to the magical moments they had shared over the Christmas period. She longed to linger in that warmth, cherishing every waking moment with Jack, but reality loomed large, reminding her that this dream could not last forever.

The uncertainty weighed heavily on Lucy's heart. Jack hadn't mentioned when he would be back, and the thought of his absence tugged at her, stirring a deep yearning within her chest. Two months felt like an eternity, and each day without him was a reminder of how much she truly missed him.

Then, opportunity knocked when she was scheduled to travel to Scotland for work. With her birthday approaching, Lucy's employer had graciously booked her an extra night in a hotel, giving her the perfect chance to explore the scenic wonders of Scotland with Jack. Excitement bubbled within her as she imagined the landscapes of emerald hills and cascading waterfalls, now seemingly within reach. She couldn't wait to share the wonderful news with him.

But when she called Jack that evening, the warmth of her excitement met an unexpected chill in his response. His voice held a note of irritation, hinting at annoyance that she hadn't consulted him before making plans. It stung for a moment, yet Lucy's determination overshadowed any disappointment. After a heartfelt conversation, they began to shift their focus toward the adventure ahead. They plotted their itinerary with enthusiasm, discovering hidden gems—picturesque places to visit, with vibrant colours and the soothing sounds of nature to excite them.

The night before their departure, Jack finally returned home, his presence filling the room with a sense of comfort and familiarity. They settled in together, the soft glow of the TV casting light on their faces as they watched movies. They huddled close, wrapped in their duvet, exchanging stories and dreams while preparing for their thrilling journey that awaited them in the morning.

Chapter Sixteen

After a long, winding drive through the picturesque Scottish countryside, Lucy and Jack finally arrived in the bustling city of Glasgow. The excitement in the air was palpable, but Lucy's anticipation quickly turned bittersweet as she realised, she had to start work immediately. With a sigh, she waved goodbye to Jack, who was charged with the task of checking into their hotel room while she dove into her responsibilities.

As Jack approached the hotel, its unassuming facade did little to mask the unsettling ambiance within. The moment he stepped inside, he was met by a faint smell of dampness and the unsettling sound of raised voices filtering through the thin walls. It became increasingly clear that an argument was brewing in the room next door, leaving him feeling uneasy about their chances for a restful night. Concerned, he texted Lucy to express his worries about the noisy neighbours, sending her videos to capture the extent of the chaos.

Yet, in the midst of his frustrations, Lucy remained unfazed. For her, the only thing that truly mattered was being with Jack. She would have willingly slept in a tent in the middle of a field if it meant she could steal moments of solitude with him.

When her workday finally came to a close, Jack was waiting to whisk her away. As she stepped back into the hotel room, she couldn't help but smile sheepishly at what he had described. The tension from the arguing couple next door was now all too real, but instead of letting it dampen their spirits, they decided to make the most of the evening. Joking and laughing, they shared stories and dreams over an impromptu dinner in their cramped quarters, trying to drown out the noise with their own cheerful chatter.

Determined to find a better place for the following night, Jack assured Lucy he would happily cover the costs; he wanted her birthday to be nothing short of magical. He couldn't bear the thought of celebrating her special day in a place that felt far from ideal.

The next morning, while Lucy donned her work attire, Jack took on the mission of finding a new hotel that met his high standards. He spent the afternoon diligently searching for a suitable place, meticulously comparing options until he finally settled on one that looked promising. After booking and paying for their new accommodation, he carefully transported all their belongings, hoping for a more peaceful night.

When Lucy finished her shift, Jack whisked her away to dinner at a cosy little restaurant he had discovered. The warm ambiance was a welcome relief from the chaos of the previous night. Over delicious food, they engaged in lively conversation, sharing smiles and laughter as they recounted their separate adventures of the day. Jack spoke animatedly about the hidden gems he'd found while exploring the city, while Lucy enthusiastically recounted her experiences with the friendly Glaswegian locals, their accents a delightful melody in the otherwise bustling environment. Together, they began to create unforgettable memories, setting the stage for a lovely birthday celebration ahead.

After Lucy's work had concluded for the day, the pair set off on an adventure into the picturesque countryside, where they stumbled upon a mesmerising waterfall cascading down the rocky cliffs. The sunlight danced on the water's surface, creating a twinkling spectacle that captivated them. Drawn in by the enchanting sight, they crawled beneath the waterfall's shimmering veil, where the sound of rushing water enveloped them in a soothing embrace. With a small, smooth stone in hand, they etched their names into the cool, damp rock, a permanent testament to their bond and the beautiful day they had shared. They snapped countless pictures, eager to fill the pages of their scrapbook with memories that would last a lifetime.

However, the magic of the trip seemed to draw to a close all too quickly. Once they returned home, the atmosphere shifted as Jack, looking a bit weary yet unwavering, broke the news that he had to return to work the next day. Lucy's heart sank, a wave of anger washing over her like a storm. "Why would he choose now, of all times, to leave me, just a day before my birthday?" she thought, frustration boiling inside her. What started as disappointment escalated into a heated argument; Jack's insistence on his responsibilities clashed with Lucy's longing for connection. She felt abandoned, hurt that he was dismissing the significance of her special day, while Jack felt increasingly frustrated by Lucy's reaction, believing she was downplaying the precious time they had just spent together.

The night air thickened with their unresolved emotions; each word exchanged only fuelling the fire of discontent. Finally, Jack relented and agreed to postpone his departure until the following day, but his words stung: "You're not a child anymore, Lucy." Each syllable cut deep; Lucy felt a wave of sadness sweep over her. They had often reminisced about how Johnathon had never valued her in the way she wished to be cherished. All she wanted was to feel important to someone, but this argument had only left her feeling more isolated.

The morning light crept through the window as Jack prepared to leave, and Lucy's heart ached with unspoken words. Desperate for an outlet for her feelings yet hesitant to voice them, she refrained from confiding in anyone, fearing they might view Jack unfavourably. She chose to keep her struggles private, unwilling to let one heated disagreement tarnish their relationship. Deep down, Lucy understood that love is often tested, and she remained hopeful that their bond would withstand this storm, trusting that they would navigate through it together.

The next few months stretched out like an endless road, the distance between Lucy and Jack growing palpable despite their regular phone calls. Each conversation felt bittersweet, a reminder of the closeness they once shared. As Jack travelled away from home, Lucy threw herself into her life, spending long hours with Dale and her friends, trying to fill the void with laughter and distractions. Yet, beneath the surface, a sense of discomfort settled in her chest—it was as if a shadow loomed over her heart whenever she thought of Jack being so far away.

When Jack finally returned home, a wave of relief washed over Lucy, calming the storm of anxiety that had brewed within her during his absence. For reasons she couldn't quite articulate, the uneasiness that had plagued her faded away as soon as she saw him. Their reunion felt electric, igniting the romantic spark that had dimmed in Jack's absence. They resumed their cherished routine of regular date nights, filled with cinematic adventures and candlelit dinners that felt imbued with love. They meandered through picturesque countryside, revelling in the beauty of nature; the crisp air and vibrant landscapes invigorated their spirits. It became a fleeting escape where they jumped into crystal-clear waters beneath majestic waterfalls, with Jack wrapping his arms around Lucy to keep her afloat—a protective embrace that felt reassuring.

Life unfolded beautifully, tinged with joy and laughter, and visions of a shared future in Canada painted their conversations with excitement. They spoke of dreams and adventures, weaving plans together like stitches of hope. Though discussions about a wedding remained scarce, Jack's endearing habit of calling Lucy his fiancée ignited a flame of anticipation within her—each mention felt like a promise of something wonderful waiting on the horizon.

However, as the weeks passed, cracks began to surface beneath their rekindled romance. Despite the laughter and joy, they found themselves slipping into petty arguments that seemed to erupt from nowhere. The air would fill with tension, and in the aftermath, Jack would often retreat, disappearing into the demands of work, leaving disputes unresolved and Lucy feeling an unsettling void. This nagging anxiety festered within her; an insidious whisper suggested that perhaps Jack had found someone else to confide in, someone who could ease the burdens he carried.

Each time Jack offered little reassurance; it only fanned the flames of her insecurities. She began to spiral into despair, feeling as if she was slowly losing Jack to an unknown rival—a faceless figure that haunted her thoughts and dreams. It was a fear she had never experienced before, a profound shift in their relationship dynamics that left her feeling unmoored. The love that once felt so vibrant now danced precariously on the edge, and Lucy couldn't shake the feeling that something was irrevocably changing between them.

Finally, after months of tension and uncertainty, Lucy and Jack sat down for an open heart-to-heart. The weight of unspoken grievances hung heavily in the air, but Jack took a deep breath and initiated the conversation. He looked into Lucy's eyes, determination etched on his face, as he expressed his willingness to change the behaviours that had been sowing seeds of anxiety in her heart. Lucy, feeling the flood of emotions coursing through her, nodded in agreement. She knew that her fears of cheating and betrayal had been poisoning their relationship, and it was time to let go of those accusations. Together, they decided to draw a line under all their bickering, resolved to start anew.

The air between them lightened, and a profound sense of relief enveloped Lucy. She felt as if a heavy fog had lifted, revealing the sun-drenched path they once walked together, filled with laughter and love. The exhilarating prospect of rekindling their romance made her heart race. Jack returned to his endearing habit of surprising her with beautiful bouquets, vibrant with the colours of spring, while Lucy found her voice again, offering heartfelt compliments and creating a relaxed atmosphere filled with warmth whenever they were together.

One evening, as Jack was immersed in his work, Lucy settled into their cosy living room, sipping a cup of coffee and reflecting on how far they had come. But in the midst of that quiet moment, an unsettling thought pierced through her contentment—she had missed her period. Panic surged within her, tightening her chest. This wasn't something they had planned for; their lives had only just began to feel stable again.

The next day, with a mix of trepidation and curiosity, she ventured out to the local supermarket and purchased a pregnancy test. As she walked through the aisles, the fluorescent lights flickered overhead, adding to her growing anxiety. She felt torn inside, unsure whether to hope for or fear the result, given the delicate state of their relationship.

It took her most of the day to muster the courage to confront the reality of the test. Finally, she found herself in their bathroom, heart pounding, fingers trembling as she followed the instructions. She set a timer on her phone, the anticipation crawling by agonisingly slowly. Three minutes felt like an eternity, each tick of the clock amplifying her anxiety and uncertainty.

When the timer finally chimed, Lucy reached for the test, her breath hitching in her throat. As she glanced down at the small plastic stick, disbelief washed over her as two red lines emerged vividly against the stark white background. She was pregnant. The realisation sent a whirlwind of emotions crashing over her—joy, fear, anxiety, and overwhelming uncertainty about how to break the news to Jack. A wave of panic washed over her at the thought of how he might react. Her heart sank at the prospect of their fragile peace being shattered again. Ideally, she would have preferred to share this life-altering news with him in person, but with Jack still absorbed in his work, she knew that wasn't an option. The prospect of finding the right words felt nearly insurmountable, leaving her hovering on the brink of a decision that could change everything.

Lucy sat on the sofa, the faint glow of her phone illuminating her anxious face. She knew she needed to send a message to Jack to share the life-altering news she had just discovered, but every time she attempted to type out her feelings, the words felt clumsy and inadequate. Her fingers hovered over the screen, typing and deleting messages that failed to capture the weight of the moment. Frustration welled up inside her as she hit the backspace key once more, erasing yet another attempt that just didn't feel right.

After what seemed like an eternity, Lucy realised that trying to find the perfect words was futile. Instead, she decided to take a picture of the test. The small, simple image seemed to carry so much more meaning than any sentence she could muster. With a deep breath, she snapped the photo and sent it off to Jack, her heart racing with both fear and hope.

Time felt stretched as she waited for a response, each second dragging on like an hour. Finally, her phone buzzed to life, and tension gripped her as she opened Jack's message. He was confused, questioning the significance of the photo she had sent. Lucy felt a mixture of anxiety and urgency wash over her as she typed out a response, her heart pounding in her chest as she revealed the truth: she was pregnant.

His reaction was palpable through the screen; she could almost sense his shock radiating out to her. The silence that followed was deafening, neither of them quite knowing what to say. They volleyed texts back and forth, their words a blend of uncertainty and tentative excitement. Finally, Jack broke the back-and-forth rhythm, his message ringing true with sincerity: he was happy if she was happy.

In that moment, a wave of relief crashed over Lucy, washing away her fears. Jack continued, expressing his desire to be a father, his words warming her heart. The weight of the news that had kept her in knots melted away, replaced by a shared sense of hope and joy, binding them together in this new chapter of their lives.

As they spoke on the phone, their laughter and whispers wove through the stillness of the night, each word deepening the bond they shared. Lucy felt the warmth of Jack's voice enveloping her, a connection that pulsed with heartfelt promises. In that intimate moment, she let herself dream of the new life they envisioned together, a life filled with hope and possibility.

Her heart swelled as she reflected on the journey that had brought them to this point—a journey entwined with love, struggles, and now, the anticipation of a little miracle growing inside her. It was a tiny heartbeat, yet it resonated with the power of their love.

Lucy gazed into Jack's eyes on her screen, filled with a depth of understanding and devotion that made her pulse quicken. She had always wanted him; he was her compass, guiding her through life's storms. But now, with this delicate new life nestled within her, she realised she had been given so much more than she had ever hoped for.

In that serene moment, as silence enveloped them, Lucy made a heartfelt decision. Sometimes, she mused, dreams don't just exist in the realm of wishes—they bloom into reality, taking shape in the warm embrace of love and the beauty of possibility. And there, in the quiet of the night, she understood that her dreams were unfolding before her, vibrantly and undeniably true.